"I won't let go of you, Annis!"

Jake's voice was placidly matter-of-fact. There had been nothing about it to set her heart pounding and sudden chaotic thoughts racing through her head.

In that moment Annis knew it wasn't Ola she loved; he meant nothing at all. Only Jake's enormous arm holding her safe, and his quiet, reassuring voice seemed important.

There would never be anyone else, she knew that now. Even in the shock of her discovery the truth stood out like a huge milestone and couldn't be denied.

But in the same moment the whole glorious wonder of it was doused by the knowledge that Dr. Jake van Germert wasn't even faintly interested in her. And besides, once she left the station she would never see him again!

OTHER
Harlequin Romances
by BETTY NEELS

Midnight Sun's Magic

by

BETTY NEELS

Harlequin Books

TORONTO·LONDON·NEW YORK·AMSTERDAM
SYDNEY·HAMBURG·PARIS·STOCKHOLM

Original hardcover edition published in 1979
by Mills & Boon Limited

ISBN 0-373-02314-6

Harlequin edition published February 1980

Printed in U.S.A.

CHAPTER ONE

THE din on the ward was unbelievable, rising and falling like a stormy sea gone mad; children calling to
each other, crying, screaming, shouting from their cots
and beds, while those already up and dressed and able
to eat their breakfast at the miniature table in the
centre of the ward were darting up and down, evading
the nurses trying to tie their bibs and settle them to
their porridge, and accompanying these sounds was the
constant thin cry of the babies in the side wards, wanting their next feed, the whole cemented together by
the rattle of spoons in bowls and the thumping of
mugs.

The young woman who had opened the door on to
this uproar closed her eyes for a split second and a tiny
frown marred her lovely features, but it was banished
instantly as she opened them again, remarkable dark
green eyes with long curling lashes, made all the more
remarkable by the rich chestnut of her hair. She was a
tall girl with a figure as striking as her face and she
held herself well; her friends considered her to be a
beauty, while the few who weren't referred to her
grudgingly as handsome, implying that she was too big
and opulent for beauty. She paused now just inside the
door and surveyed the ward with a practised eye; she
had been Sister on the Children's Ward at Anselm's
for three years now and had grown accustomed to the

turmoil around her, and she could see now that everything was just as it should be. She waved to the children at the table and without pausing again went straight to her office where the night nurses would be waiting.

With the report given and the pair of them gone, she re-read it, made up the day book so that each nurse knew what she had to do, glanced at the off duty book and was on the point of getting up from her desk when her staff nurse, Carol Drew, came in. She was a small, neat girl, devoted to her work, and they got on splendidly together.

She smiled as she came in, said 'Good morning, Sister,' and waited.

'Morning, Carol—and for heaven's sake stop calling me Sister when there's no one around. I see Archie's been sick twice. We'd better get Mr Potter to go over him again—we've missed something ...' She stretched out a hand for the telephone. 'And Night Nurse says that Baby Scott isn't feeding—he'd better have a look at her too. Is there anything else to worry us?' She sighed. 'I've an idea we're in for a bad day.'

Carol nodded her head. 'Me too—Baby Cook's ready for theatre.'

'I'll take him up—I've just time to do a round first. How is breakfast going?'

Her staff nurse cast her eyes upwards. 'The usual; we're just starting to clear up the mess, I'll go and see how they're getting on.' At the door she looked back. 'I say, Annis, don't you want to be here when Mr Potter comes?'

Annis Brown raised her magnificent head from the papers she was studying. 'No, I don't,' she grinned, and looked much younger than her twenty-seven years. 'You can have him.'

But she didn't smile when Carol had left her. Arthur Potter was becoming a problem in her life; he was persistent in his wish to marry her, worthy to the point of being boring, an excellent doctor with an undoubtedly successful career before him and one of the dullest young men she had ever met. They had known each other for three years now and he was beginning to grow on her so that every now and then the unwelcome thought that she would eventually marry him was becoming increasingly difficult to dispel; the trouble was that she liked him as a friend—he was kind and considerate and non-demanding, he had an even temper and looked upon her occasional outburst with tolerance, and she found herself wishing more and more frequently that he might display some temper himself, or at least disagree with her.

The trouble was that she didn't know what she wanted; to get married, of course, to remain a Ward Sister all her life had no appeal for her; she wanted a home and a husband and children of her own, but she hadn't met anyone who had swept her off her feet and she was beginning to doubt if she ever would. She sighed and went into the ward, to become immediately engrossed in the sick little people who lived in it.

She went first to the table where the convalescents were eating the last of their breakfasts and sat down with them, idly eating a slice of bread and butter while she enquired as to how they felt; not that she was hungry, but she had discovered long ago that reluctant eaters were inclined to eat a slice with her while they talked and shouted and cried. Little Betty Wakes, the coeliac disease who had been with them for so long, she took on to her lap, comforting her while she grizzled—she grizzled a lot and from Annis's point of view, she had every reason to do so. Presently, when she had discovered all she wanted to know about the children round the table, she carried Betty round the ward with her, stopping by each cot and small bed, reading charts, casting a knowledgeable eye over each occupant and occasionally pausing to speak to one or other of the nurses. It took her all of half an hour and she was back in her office just in time to meet Arthur Potter as he came along the corridor.

He was a tall thin young man, with hair already receding from a clever forehead, and his glasses emphasised his earnest manner. He greeted her gravely, reminded her that they were going out together that evening, and then became absorbed in Archie's charts. By the time he had asked a few questions and pondered the symptoms it was time for Annis to gather up Baby Cook and bear him off to theatre for his pyloric stenosis to be corrected. He was a very small baby, and wizened through insufficient nourishment, but Annis kissed the top of the elderly little head, assured the infant that he would be as beautiful as any baby that lived in no time at all, a remark which Arthur, who had caught up with her in the ward, gently but seriously pointed out wasn't quite accurate. Baby Cook would never be beautiful, however well fed he was; his eyes were small and squinted slightly, his hair was sparse and dull and his mouth too large. Annis told the doctor quite fiercely that he knew nothing about it, and sped away.

Baby Cook was to be done first. Annis stayed in theatre, giving a helping hand to the anaesthetist while the surgeons worked, and presently, when their work was finished, she picked up the small creature and bore him gently back to a side ward where one or other of her more senior student nurses would special him for the next twenty-four hours.

Annis laid him gently on to his cot, glanced at her watch and said: 'We'll start feeds in—let me see—three and three-quarter hours from now—four mls of glucose, nurse, and then two-hourly feeds alternating with glucose. I'll let you know when to increase them and I want to know at once if he brings them up.' She smiled at the girl, gave a final look at Master Cook and sailed away to superintend the dressings.

She had been right, the day was busy and full of small setbacks, so that by the time she got off duty that evening the last thing she wanted to do was go out with Arthur. There must be something wrong with her, she mused; they were such good friends and on the whole she enjoyed being with him, although she was honest enough to admit to herself that he bored her a little more each time she went out with him. No, not bored, she corrected herself. Everything they did together was done from habit, there was no excitement —surely, if she were in love with him, even the littlest bit, she would feel a thrill at meeting him, spending the evening with him, even seeing him on the ward? It was like putting on an old coat one was particularly fond of—it might do nothing for one, but it was comfortable. She frowned and poked around in her wardrobe, trying to decide what to wear. Something different, she decided, something to make Arthur look at her—really look at her. There was a dress she had bought at a sale some months back; it had looked lovely in the window, but when she had got it home it had been too daringly cut. Mindful of Arthur's views on modesty in women, she had hung it at the back of her more discreet clothes and forgotten about it. Now some imp of mischief made her decide to wear it. It was a pretty colour, soft misty blue, and the material was pretty too, but the neckline was quite outrageous. All the same, she put it on, did her lovely face, allowed her hair to fall free and went down to the hospital entrance, prudently wrapped in a light coat.

'You'll be too warm,' advised Arthur the moment he saw her. 'It's mid-May, you know.'

She assured him that she wouldn't and climbed into the car—a Triumph, kept in tip-top condition and treated with care. A race down a motorway wasn't in Arthur's line, he preferred to do a steady fifty in the slow lane because it was better for the engine and didn't use as much petrol, and in London now he travelled very slowly indeed. Annis who drove well if rather recklessly herself, reminded herself that Arthur was a good, steady driver who would never take risks. He would be a good steady husband too. She sighed and he asked at once: 'Had a busy day? Children can be the very devil sometimes.' He glanced sideways at her. 'You and I will have had enough of them by the time we settle down.'

Annis, a good-tempered girl, gritted her splendid

teeth, contemplating a lifetime ahead of her settling down in a pristine house with not a single child to muddy the floor or scuff the paint. How dull the future looked, and really it was so silly. She had no need to marry Arthur; it was simply that circumstances had thrown them continuously together for the last three years—besides, he hadn't asked her, only taken it for granted that she would. Well, she wouldn't. 'Arthur ...' she began.

'I prefer not to talk while I'm driving in town,' he reminded her kindly. 'I daresay it's something that can wait until we're at the restaurant.'

But once sitting at the table with him, she found it impossible. He was being at his nicest; considerate, thoughtful of her every wish, keeping the conversation pleasant. It was over the coffee that he asked her: 'What was it you wanted to ask me, Annis?'

It was her chance, but she couldn't take it after all, he looked so kind—so she shook her head and said that it didn't matter.

But after a more or less sleepless night, she knew that she would have to do something about it, and the opportunity occurred sooner than she expected. Arthur had done a round with Mr Travers, the paediatrician, and stayed behind to write up fresh instructions on some of the charts. He sat at Annis's desk while she altered the day book, perched on the only other chair in the little room, and presently, almost finished, he sat back and put his pen down.

'That was rather a sexy dress you wore last night,' he observed in a mildly reproving voice. 'I can't say that I entirely approve.'

'You noticed it—that's something, anyway. I've thought that just lately you don't see me any more, only in the same way as you see your breakfast porridge or—or your stethoscope or pen ...' She went on crossly: 'As to approving, it's none of your business what I choose to wear.'

He looked surprised and vaguely displeased, but before he could say anything she went on, getting crosser every minute: 'Arthur, do you intend to marry me?'

The displeasure was no longer vague. 'My dear Annis, surely that's a question which I should ask you?'

She had the bit well and truly between her teeth now. 'Well, why don't you?'

'These things can't be rushed,' he told her with a patient tolerance which sent her temper soaring even higher. "We're two busy people, we aren't able to see each other as much as some men and women do—we have to get to know each other ...'

She gaped at him. If you didn't know someone with whom you worked each day and spent a good deal of your leisure with for the best part of three years, surely you should give it up as a bad job? And what about love, she thought confusedly—falling in love? Surely that came in a blinding flash all of a sudden, not after months of lukewarm affection? If Arthur had been in love with her, really in love, probably she would have married him even though she felt nothing but a deep regard for him. As it was she could see now, very clearly indeed, that she could never marry him. Even if she never married, she wouldn't regret it. She said now: 'I'm not the right wife for you, Arthur. I know we're good friends and we've got used to seeing each other every day, but that's not enough, not for me, anyway.'

He had picked up a chart and had his pen poised to write. 'If that's how you feel about it, Annis, then there's no more to be said, is there?'

She couldn't refrain from asking him: 'Don't you mind?'

He thought carefully before he answered. 'Yes, at the moment I mind. I'd woven you into the pattern of my future ...'

'Yes, but the present, Arthur—never mind the future!'

He looked surprised. 'But the future matters, Annis. I must make a success of it; do exactly what I've planned.'

'Did you plan me into it, then?'

'Oh, yes—later on.'

'But I'm twenty-seven, Arthur!'

'Another three or four years and we could have discussed marriage,' he told her comfortably. 'Neither of us, I fancy, would want children—our life would have been too busy.' He smiled at her kindly. 'If you like, we'll forget the whole of this conversation.'

She wanted to cry, a mixture of rage and sorrow, she supposed miserably. 'No, Arthur, I don't want to forget it. We've—we've had a very pleasant friendship and I'm sure you'll find someone exactly right for you.'

One who'll wait patiently until he has his life exactly as he wants it and can fit a wife in without it interfering, she thought, and said out loud:

'What shall we do about Archie? Do you suppose he's cooking up something nasty?'

She could see the relief on his face as he began on the pros and cons of operating on Archie.

She wasn't off duty until eight o'clock that evening and she didn't mind; after a busy day she would be too tired to do more than have her supper, a bath, and then in her dressing gown, sit for a while drinking tea in one or other of the Sisters' bedrooms.

An arrangement which didn't mature. True, she got off duty and had her supper, but on her way over to the Home, Dodge, the head porter, singled her out from the little group crossing the entrance hall and handed her a letter.

'Came this evening,' he told her, 'and got overlooked, Sister. I was just going to send it over to the Home.'

She recognised her brother's writing and the Norwegian stamp as she took it, pushed it idly into a pocket, thanked Dodge and ran to catch up the others. Freddy wrote spasmodically and infrequently and although they were a devoted brother and sister, she had long ago given up getting him to do otherwise. He was a few years younger than she and a clever atomic engineer whose work took him all over the world. At the moment he was in Spitzbergen, working with a team in some remote spot and glad to be there, for earlier in the year he had broken off his engagement to a girl Annis had privately considered not at all suitable for him to marry, and was mending a supposedly broken heart among the snow and ice and no girls for miles around. Annis, knowing him well, guessed that by the time he returned to civilisation he would be ready to fall in love all over again.

There was something worth seeing on the T.V. some-one had offered and she went with the rest of them, to crowd round the box in the rather small, stuffy room which they all shared. It was mild for the time of year and still light, and in between watching they discussed summer clothes and holidays. Annis, listening to her friends arguing about the various places they would like to visit, wondered what she would do. There was Great-Aunt Mary at Mere, of course, always glad to see her or Freddy, for they were all the family she had and she had left it rather late to arrange anything else, for she had the first two weeks of her holidays in a month's time when it would be the middle of June. She sighed a little and remembered her letter.

Freddy wrote briefly; he was never one to waste time on letters anyway. She read the few lines in a moment or two and then read them again, very slowly this time. Freddy wanted her to join him—the cook-cum-secretary-cum-nurse who was attached to the team had been flown back to Oslo with appendicitis and he had immediately thought of her to fill the gap and offered to get her there as quickly as possible. 'It's time you had a change,' he wrote, cheerfully impervious to things like giving in her notice and whether she wanted to go anyway, 'it's almost summer here and you'll love it—no real hard work and you couldn't meet a nicer bunch of chaps than the team. Wire me when you in-tend to arrive. We can manage for a week or two, but make it sooner than that if you can. Will send informa-tion about how to reach us when I hear from you; send a radiogram.'

Her first impulse was to dismiss the whole thing as

one of Freddy's scatterbrained ideas. It was Nora Kemp, Sister on Women's Surgical and a great friend of Annis, who asked her why she looked so surprised and when Annis told her, said at once: 'But of course you must go! What a chance—you could always get taken back on the staff here, but I bet no one will ever ask you to go to Spitzbergen again. I wish he'd asked me.'

'But they would want me at once—or in a week at most.'

Everyone was listening now and several voices joined in. 'You've got holidays due,' said someone, 'three weeks, isn't it? Well, you can give notice and leave at the end of the week. No reason why you shouldn't— family matters, you know, and you've got Carol Drew as Staff, haven't you? She's quite able to step into your shoes.'

It was Peggy Trevitt, Junior Sister on Casualty, who offered slyly: 'Perhaps Annis doesn't want to go— Arthur might object.'

Annis shook her head. 'Why should he?' she wanted to know coolly. She didn't like Peggy all that much.

'Well, of course if you only went for a few weeks,' conceded Peggy.

'I've been thinking of a change, anyway,' declared Annis, who hadn't given the idea a thought until that moment. 'I think perhaps I'll go.'

That triggered off a lively discussion as to the clothes she should take with her and how she should get there.

'By plane?' asked Nora. 'But is there anywhere where one can land up there? Surely it's all rocks and mountains and ice ...'

'Boat?' ventured Annis. 'I don't even know if people actually live there.'

'Well, you soon will ...' There was a good deal of laughter. 'You'll need a fur coat, Annis, and those hideous boots that look like bedsocks—and thick woolly undies ...'

'It's summer there,' observed Annis, 'Freddy said something about getting tanned.' She got up. 'Well, I shall sleep on it. Perhaps Miss Phipps won't let me go in a week's time.'

But Miss Phipps, surprisingly, did. She was reluctant to let Annis go, of course, for she would be losing a good nurse, but she had expected to do that anyway and she was only surprised that Annis wanted to leave for a reason other than marrying Arthur Potter. Like her lesser colleagues, she had watched the affair blossom, although she had considered privately that the parties concerned were taking far too long to make up their minds, and now, looking at the beautiful creature standing in front of her desk, she felt a vague relief. Annis Brown was far too good for him. Perhaps if she went on this expedition or whatever it was, she would meet someone who could match her in looks and not take her for granted like Mr Potter did. Miss Phipps thought that in Sister Brown's place she would most certainly have gone herself—it sounded most interesting and a little unusual, and she was a sensible girl as well as being a beautiful one. Miss Phipps, conjuring up rather inaccurate mental pictures of the Spitzbergen landscape, felt a distinct touch of envy.

Having made up her mind, Annis didn't waste time. She sent a radiogram to Freddy, asking for directions as to how to get there, bought slacks and an assortment of blouses and sweaters, a new parka, some sensible shoes and a supply of cosmetics; Freddy had said that the country looked lovely, but he had never mentioned shops. She added a book or two, and obedient to the instructions which Freddy sent by return, booked on a flight to Tromso where she would be met. That left her with exactly a day in which to visit Great-Aunt Mary.

She left London very early in the morning, having said her goodbyes on the previous day, and that had included a rather uncomfortable ten minutes with Arthur. He had been rather superior about it all, treating it as a joke and declaring in his calm way that she would probably hate the whole set-up when she got there. 'I might even renew our very pleasant relationship when you return, as most certainly you will.' He had smiled at her and for a brief moment she wondered if she was being a complete fool, but she had pushed the idea away at once, feeling resentful at his smugness. And now in the train she wasn't thinking about him at all, she was thinking with regret of the ward she had left; all the funny, noisy, pathetic children and babies who lived in it, however briefly. She would miss them; she would miss her friends too; she had made a great many during her years in hospital. She settled back in her seat and picked up the morning paper. There was no point in getting sentimental, she told herself firmly.

It was a two-hour journey to Gillingham, the nearest station to Mere. Only a handful of people got out there; a small, pleasant country town where the ticket collector had time to smile and say good morning as they filed out of the station. Great-Aunt Mary was out-side at the wheel of the Morris 1000 which she had bought years ago and didn't intend to change. 'It will last as long as I shall,' she had declared to a car sales-man who had done his best to persuade her to trade it in for a more modern car, 'and that's more than can be said for a great many motor cars put on the market these days, young man.'

She waved to Annis now and then put her head through the window to say: 'Put everything in the trunk, dear, I shall need the back for the groceries.'

She offered a sunburnt cheek for Annis to kiss and took a good look at her. 'London doesn't suit you. I'm glad you're going on this trip with Freddy, it sounds a most unusual set-up, but then I never have pretended to understand these modern atomic things ...'

'I think it's electronics, too,' murmured Annis.

'All one and the same,' declared Great-Aunt Mary largely, 'but I should think that part of the world should be rather interesting.'

She was driving at a stately pace along the crown of the road, taking no notice of those who would like to overtake and couldn't. 'Who's meeting you when you get there?'

'I don't know,' said Annis. 'I hope it's Freddy, then he can tell me a bit about it. I don't even know how long I'm to be there.'

'A nice change from living to a timetable. It'll do you good, my dear—another year or two at that hospital and you would have been an old maid, whether you'd married that Arthur fellow or not.'

Annis didn't answer that, for it was very probably

true; she said instead: 'Well, I am looking forward to it. Are you stopping at Walton's?'

'Only to pick up a few things they'll have ready for me. Do you really have to go back this evening?'

'Yes, Aunt. The plane goes very early in the morning—I'm spending the night at an hotel close by the airport—my case is there already.'

Great-Aunt Mary had slowed down as they entered the village, swung round the corner between the two local pubs, and stopped before the grocer's.

'What clothes are you taking?' she wanted to know. She was a poor dresser herself; she had a short, plump figure which she declared nothing off the peg fitted, and she was right, but that didn't stop her loving clothes. They talked about them while the groceries were loaded, and didn't pause when she drove on presently to stop a few hundred yards further, pull into a side road and stop.

They walked from the car to the cottage, carrying the groceries between them, down a narrow path running beside a clear stream and crossed at intervals by little bridges leading to the back gardens on the other side.

Great-Aunt Mary's cottage had a bridge too, leading to a tiny triangle of grass and flowers which fronted her home; a red brick Victorian cottage, its side wall rising straight out of the stream with windows opening on to it. It was bigger inside than it looked from the lane—true, the hall was narrow but the staircase was nicely placed and the dining room and what its owner called the drawing room were a fair size, and to make up for the Lilliputian kitchen, there were innumerable cupboards, big enough to house a piano if needed. Annis loved it; she had lived there for a few years after her parents died, going as a weekly boarder to Sherborne School for Girls while Freddy had gone to Bryanston, coming home for school holidays, and she had always returned for holidays all the time she had been at St Anselm's. She looked around her now, at the white walls hung with a wide variety of pictures, some really good, some framed cards which her aunt had taken a fancy to, at the old-fashioned furniture which fitted so well into the Victorian appearance of the little place and the windows with their pretty chintz curtains. 'It's nice to be home,' she said.

It was over lunch that Great-Aunt Mary remarked suddenly: 'Of course, I should very much have preferred it if you had been getting married, though not to Arthur. You're twenty-seven, aren't you, Annis?' she eyed her niece's splendid figure across the table, 'and there can't be all that number of men in the world to match up to you.'

'Match up to me?' asked Annis faintly.

'Looks, my dear, and height, and come to that, size. You're hardly *petite*, are you? Perhaps there'll be someone suitable among the Norwegians.'

Annis giggled. 'I'll keep an eye open.' she promised.

She left early that evening with regret. The little house looked delightful in the late sunshine and the hills around were turning to golden. Snow and ice, she thought—I must be mad!

But due reflection made it obvious to her that it was rather less mad to go traipsing off to the top of the world than to continue the lukewarm and far too cautious relationship with Arthur. At least Spitzbergen was different, or she hoped it would be; indeed, the more she thought about it the better she liked the idea. She slept soundly on it, ate a good breakfast and arrived, unruffled and very neat, in good time for her flight.

She had flown before, but only short flights, and she was disappointed to find that the journey was over so quickly. She had expected that the six-hour trip would have given her plenty of time to look at the passing world beneath her, but what with take-off and coffee and then, just as she was picking out the coastline below, lunch, she had very little time to peer out of her porthole. They were landing before she had had more than a glimpse of Tromso, on the islands below her, hugging Norway's rugged coast.

Freddy was waiting for her and although she was a girl well able to look after herself, she was more than pleased to see him. There were any number of questions she wanted answered too.

'Not now, Sis, I've got a company plane waiting to take off.'

'Oh, don't we have any time at all here? A cup of tea ...?'

He grinned. 'They'll wait that long. Come on, over here, just stand there while I get someone to take your luggage.'

It wasn't tea, but coffee, strong and dark, accompanied by large, satisfying buns. 'How long does it take?' asked Annis, her mouth full.

'It's eight hundred miles—about three hours; as it

doesn't get dark at all we don't have to worry about landing.'

'Oh, but how shall we ...?'

Freddy was on his feet. 'We'll have to go—there'll be plenty of time to talk later.'

She had expected that they would return to the airfield, but Freddy got into a small Saab with the driver already at the wheel and she got in with him, prudently asking no more questions. There was plenty to keep her occupied. Tromso was delightful with the forest all around it, joined to the mainland by a long bridge, its wooden houses gay with flowers, and having an air of happy bustle. There were ships of all sorts in its harbour, too, and she looked at Freddy, a little puzzled; he had said a plane ...

'Out there,' he said laconically, and nodded towards a seaplane a few hundred yards out. The Saab stopped and Annis found herself being ushered into a small boat, her luggage piled in after her and Freddy beside her while the driver started the outboard motor; she barely had time to take a last lingering look at Tromso before she was clambering on board.

There was already someone there, a slight young man, who grinned at her with an easy 'Hullo—so Freddy found you.' He whistled: 'And aren't you a lovely surprise—hefty,' he added, 'strong as a horse and never turns a hair.' He put out a hand. 'I'm Jeff Blake, I do the book work and sometimes I'm allowed to pilot the plane—this one, that is, not Jake's.'

Annis laughed at him, told Freddy that he was a wretch and added: 'But I am as strong as a horse, you know.'

Jeff gave her a wicked look. 'Never mind the strength, just so long as you can bathe a fevered brow and cook.' He turned to Freddy. 'All set? Let's go, then.'

The two men talked shop, quite unintelligible to Annis, but she didn't mind. This trip was so much more exciting than the flight from London that morning; the Norwegian coast quickly disappeared and there was nothing but the sea below and the clear sky all around. She sat quietly, mulling over her day. It had all happened too quickly for her, she would have to go back to Tromso and take time to explore—which reminded her about things like days off . . .

'Do I get any free time?' she asked, ruthlessly cutting in on electronic jargon.

'Lord, yes,' Freddy assured her. 'There are only twenty of us, you know, and most of the time we're fighting fit; all we want are three good meals a day, some help with the books and a soothing hand if we're ill.' He turned to pick up a Thermos flask. 'And Jake sees to it that we never are. He doesn't mind the odd accident, but he draws the line at headaches and vague disorders.'

'And who is this Jake?'

'The doctor—the company needed one while we were at the radio station and he fancied a holiday.' He grinned at her. 'Wait till you meet him.'

'Oh—why?'

But Jeff only laughed, it was Freddy who observed: 'They'll make a good pair.'

Annis forgot their remarks soon enough. Her first glimpse of Spitzbergen dispelled every other thought from her head; great grey snow-capped mountains on the horizon, a little frightening because suddenly she realised how far they were from everywhere else. 'It looks bleak,' she ventured.

'It's beautiful, so quiet you can hear the ice floes cracking on their way through the fjords down to the sea, birds of course and seals, and the odd whale.'

'People?'

'The odd thousand or so scattered between the three settlements. And us, of course.'

'Are we very far from a—a settlement?'

'An hour's flight—someone goes once a fortnight to pick up provisions and post; the Coastal Express calls too with the odd crate.'

She had to be content with that. The men fell to talking technicalities once more, leaving her to contemplate the awe-inspiring landscape.

The sun was still shining brilliantly as Jeff brought the seaplane down close to a flat, lichen-covered tongue of rock, the mountains towered all round them with a narrow strip of rock between them and the sea, and scattered along it were wooden huts and what Annis vaguely supposed to be wireless stations; there was a round building too, standing well away from the rest. It looked remarkably lonely even in the late evening sun, but not for long. As they came to rest on the iron grey water she could see men emerging from the huts and running towards them. Two of them got into a small motorboat tied to a rickety pier and started towards the plane.

'We're here,' said Freddy unnecessarily.

There was nothing lacking in her welcome; any

doubts Annis might have still been harbouring were drowned in the enthusiastic greeting she got from the men. There were more than a dozen of them, shaking her by the hand the moment she stepped rather gingerly on the rock, telling her their names, declaring that she was the answer to a prayer—just what the doctor had ordered.

'I wasn't aware that I had done any such thing,' drawled a voice behind her, and to the accompaniment of shouts of laughter Annis turned round, bristling a little because the voice had held mockery.

Its owner suited the scenery very well. He was large and rugged, with great shoulders and towering over everyone there. Good-looking too, only his dark eyes were cool and his mouth was a thought too straight for her liking. Not so very young either, she decided; his thick dark hair was grey at the temples.

She held out a hand. 'How do you do?' she said in her sweetest voice.

CHAPTER TWO

THE hand which grasped hers was hard and firm and cool, and when she looked at the doctor's face she could see no trace of mockery there; she must have imagined it.

He said in a deep slow voice: 'Hullo, Annis, I'm so glad you have come—we've been taking it in turns to cook and we're all very bad at it.'

She said with a touch of frost because he had called her Annis without even asking: 'I'm a nurse.'

He said gravely: 'We have almost no sickness here and—we hope—only occasional accidents, but if there is a mass outbreak of measles I, and I'm sure the rest of the team—won't grumble.'

There was general laughter at that and she laughed too, not because she found it very amusing but because it was so obviously expected of her. She looked up and saw the gleam in the doctor's eye; probably he wanted to annoy her. 'I don't know your name ...' she reminded him gently.

'Jake—Jake van Germert. I hope you'll call me Jake —we're all on the best of terms; you've met most of us, but there are several on duty. You'll meet them in the morning.' He looked over the men's heads to speak to a short, fat man, a good deal older than the rest of them. 'How about Freddy taking Annis to their hut, Willy, while we dish the supper.'

She vaguely remembered shaking the fat man's hand. Presumably he was the boss; he looked mild and absent-minded and probably had a remarkable brain. He smiled at her now and came to take her arm. 'Lead on, Freddy. Annis, you can have ten minutes to make your beautiful self even more beautiful and then you shall have supper, such as it is.'

The hut, which looked bare and unwelcoming from the outside, was a surprise. Its furniture was comfortable and the covers and cushions were brightly coloured. Two rooms led from the small living room, small too, but her bed looked comfortable and there was a good sized cupboard and a dressing table. She wasn't sure what she had expected, but she was agreeably surprised now. It wasn't for a few days that she discovered that she and Freddy had been moved into the hut shared by the boss and the doctor, who had taken up quarters in one of the other huts, which while comfortable, had no living room and was more cramped. She unpacked a few things, did her hair and her face and with Freddy beside her, crossed the bare rocky ground between them and a larger hut which, he explained, was their communal centre, where they ate and played cards, and played records and spent their leisure. 'We go climbing too,' he added, 'and fishing; it's pretty quiet in the winter, though.'

The understatement of the year, thought Annis. It seemed pretty quiet now, with nothing but the seabirds calling and the gentle wash of the icy water against the rock. 'Holidays?' she asked.

'Oh, rather, everyone goes to Norway in turn—there's a plane or they can go by the Coastal Express.

I'll go in a couple of months, though; I'll be finished by then. Jake's going too—he's got a practice in Holland, you know.'

'No, I didn't know,' said Annis dryly as they went into the hut.

The men had certainly done their best. There was a long table running down the middle of the room and although there were no flowers, there were lighted candles, rather dimmed by the midnight sun but nevertheless festive. She was sat at the centre of the table, with the boss on one side and the senior engineer on the other. The doctor, she was vaguely annoyed to find, was sitting as far away as possible.

The meal was, perforce, out of tins and whoever had opened them had been lavish with the can-opener —there was more than enough for everyone and a good deal over, and Annis found it a little pathetic the way they asked her every few minutes if the food was good. She praised it lavishly, hoping her inside wouldn't rebel against the strange mixture which it was sampling. Everyone must have had a hand in preparing the meal; she worked her way through soup, cod, covered with a rich sauce which seemed to contain everything in the cookery book, a variety of vegetables, and rounded off with a steamed pudding. Over coffee they explained that they were due to fetch their stores very shortly, when she would find a much larger selection of groceries. They looked at her hopefully as they said it and she hoped that Freddy hadn't made her out to be up to Cordon Bleu standard.

They had had drinks first and wine with their meal, although she suspected that the men would have preferred beer. She was touched with their welcome, though, and resolved privately to feed them well as well as nurse them, although it seemed unlikely that there would be much of that; a tougher bunch of men she had yet to meet.

'Where did your cook come from?' she asked the boss.

'Oslo—Sven's sister ...' he nodded across the table towards a fair young man who didn't look more than twenty. 'She was a nurse too, and a typist. Do you type, Annis?'

She was glad that she could tell him that yes, she could type. 'Not very well,' she explained, 'but I'm a bit rusty at it.' Her pretty mouth curved in a smile. 'Is there an awful lot to do?'

'No, no—just once or twice a month, reports and so on, very simple.'

'You're not English?' she asked him. 'Although you speak it perfectly.'

'Finnish—we are a very mixed bunch, mostly Norwegians though, with a couple of Swedes and of course Jake, who is Dutch.'

'Yes, someone told me. What a blessing everyone speaks English, because I can't understand a word of Norwegian or Finnish or Dutch—I don't think I'd know them if I heard them.'

He laughed comfortably. 'We shall all teach you a few words and you will get quite expert.'

The dinner party broke up presently, and Annis said goodnight to everyone, thanked them prettily for her welcome and dinner and made for her hut, secretly appalled at the doctor's cool: 'Don't forget you are on duty tomorrow morning at seven o'clock, Annis. The shifts change over at eight so that the men going on duty breakfast at seven-thirty and the men coming off at eight o'clock.'

She thanked him coldly for the information. He was just the irritating kind of man to remind one of one's duty ...

The kitchen, she discovered the next morning, was remarkably up-to-date. Being a new broom she intended to sweep clean, so she was ten minutes early, making coffee, setting the table with what she hoped the men ate for breakfast. There was a huge side of bacon hanging in the larder too, but she was relieved to see that a large quantity had already been sliced. She found a frying pan as large as a football field and started frying, helped half way through by Freddy who was to go on the day shift but hadn't hurried from his bed.

'Six rashers each,' he told her. 'Just put the bread on the table—there's orange juice too.'

On the whole, Annis felt that she had acquitted herself rather well. The ten men who presently sat down to their breakfast did justice to it, complimented her on her cooking and hurried away to their various stations, all except the doctor, who had another cup of coffee, asked her rather carelessly if she had slept well, handed her a timetable of the day's work so that she knew where she was and then requested her presence in the surgery at nine o'clock. 'One of the engineers slipped early this morning and cut his leg on the rock —nothing serious, but we shall need to tidy it up a bit.'

Having said which, he took himself off, leaving her to clear the debris and get the next lot of bacon into the pan; presumably she ate with the men coming off duty. It was an agreeable surprise when two men came into the kitchen and told her that they were doing the washing up. 'We take it in turns,' they explained. 'There'll be two more for the next batch.'

They grinned at her cheerfully and eyed her with interest, while she, happily unaware of their glances, bent over the stove, unaware of the pretty picture she made. She had sensibly packed slacks and a variety of tops, and she was wearing a short-sleeved shirt over blue slacks now, enveloping the whole in a large apron she had found behind the door, a legacy from the previous cook and nurse. She hadn't bothered much with her hair, either, only brushed it out and tied it back in a ponytail. She looked considerably less than her twenty-seven years and pretty enough to eat.

The men coming off duty were tired, but they ate just as heartily as the first lot had. Annis dealt with gigantic appetites, ate her own meal and leaving two more volunteers to wash up, made her way to the surgery, a hut standing a little apart from the rest, a roomy place with a well-equipped surgery, a two-bedded ward, a portable operating table and a cupboard well stocked with instruments. The doctor was already there, bending over a man on the table. Without turning round he said: 'Ah, there you are— there's a white gown in that closet beside the door.' And as she put it on: 'Bring me that covered kidney dish, will you?'

Unfriendly to the point of being terse, she considered, and while she stood beside him, handing things, swabbing the leg, cutting gut, she had time to take a good look at him. Her first impression had been right; he was enormous and rather more heavily built than she had thought and his high-bridged nose and heavy-lidded eyes made him look ill-tempered, although that didn't seem likely, for he seemed universally popular. She wasn't sure if she was going to like him; he hadn't done so yet, but probably he was going to throw his weight about. He looked, she considered, more like a ruthless high-powered executive than a doctor. But within half an hour she found herself eating her words. The doctor, while not attempting to charm her in any way, was placidly good-natured, not saying much but responding to his patient's remarks with good-humoured patience. The injury wasn't too severe; a day or two resting it and he could return to his work in the hut at the far end of the tongue of rock. Annis was to dress it daily after the doctor had seen it. The doctor glanced at her as he spoke and smiled and she found herself smiling back at him.

She discovered within two days that the doctor was the silent one of the team. He never joined in any of the arguments or made any but the mildest of comments on any subject, yet she noticed that the men turned to him when a deciding opinion was needed, and when the argument became too fierce it was he who damped it down with a few quiet words. She wondered what he did with his day until Freddy told her that he was carrying out a series of experiments, monitoring hearts and lungs after each man came off duty as well as taking samples of everything vegetable which was living; and that wasn't much. Annis had been there for several days before she found her first flower, a minute buttercup-like plant clinging to the rock in the warm sunshine. She took care not to disturb it; it took decades for seeds to germinate in the unfriendly climate which existed for nine months of the year; each small flower was a precious thing. She was so delighted with her find that she told the doctor while she was clearing up the surgery after he had treated a boil on a Norwegian's neck, and he had told her that there were many more if she looked carefully. She waited for him to suggest that they might go together in their leisure to look for them, but in this she was disappointed. He remained silent, and she, not a vain girl but aware that she was attractive, wondered what he didn't like about her. He took almost no notice of her beyond greeting her civilly when they encountered each other about the station, making conversation when circumstances demanded it of him, and sitting at the far end of the table at meals. In a word, she told herself crossly, he was avoiding her.

And somehow this was all the more annoying when every other man there sought her out whenever she was free—trips on the sea in one of the powerful motorboats kept at the station; careful climbing expeditions to look for flowers, and when it was warm, long sessions by the sea with binoculars watching the birds and looking for seals.

The boss had taken her on a tour within a few days of her arrival; round the various huts, along to the big radio hut where the men sat at their instruments.

She had only a dim idea what they were doing and she was quick to see that no one was going to tell her anyway, although she was shown how messages were sent and how they got their electricity and the wonderful view they had of the mountains around them as well as the open sea. Cruising ships passed from time to time, she was told, on their way to the Ice Barrier and Ny Aalesund, but they never stopped at the station; for one thing, although the water was deep, the pier was only a rickety erection, liable to fall down at any minute.

'Why doesn't someone mend it, then?' asked Annis practically. She didn't wait for an answer because the Coastal Express was just in sight. It wasn't calling that day, it seemed; supplies had been brought back when she had been fetched from Tromso and as someone would be going to Ny Aalesund very shortly, the letters could be fetched from there. They trundled back to the main camp in the jeep and she went to get on with the dinner.

Her days were well filled; she was busy but not overworked and mostly the days were clear, with blue skies. There was always a boat available and someone to go with her, and when it was bad weather with ink-black clouds pressing on to the mountain tops and a cold, sullen sea, there were plenty of partners for a game of chess or backgammon. Letters to write too, a great many of them, to be taken to Ny Aalesund, the weekly film to enjoy, and books to read. She spent a good deal of time with Freddy, listening with sympathy to his account of his last love affair; he fell in and out of love so often and so briefly that she was hard put to it to remember the girl's name. She didn't think he was brokenhearted this time, though. He remembered, however, after a long monologue about girls and the last one in particular, to ask her if she were happy.

'Yes, very,' she told him, and was surprised to find that it was true. She was happy—there was very little nursing, the odd cut hand and septic finger, bruises and abrasions, but there was plenty to keep her occupied each day. She could work as she wished, no one interfered and she took her free time more or less when she liked. Only the daily surgery was strictly on time each day and although the doctor had never said a word, she made sure that she was punctual.

It was towards the end of the week when they were at supper one evening that the doctor mentioned casually that he had seen a small herd of seals further along the coast, and added: 'If you're interested, Annis, I'll show you how to reach them—it's not far if we cut across the base of the mountains. Only wear your boots.'

The invitation was given so casually that she wasn't sure if he had meant it, but when supper was finished and she had cleared the table and put everything to rights, she found him waiting, sitting on an upturned box outside the hut. It was already late evening, but there would be no night, of course; the sun shone, a rich gold, above the horizon and would stay like that until day began once more.

'Boots,' he reminded her, and she went to her hut and obediently pulled on the strong footwear she had been given on her arrival. She picked up her parka too, for the weather could change with disconcerting suddenness and she was wearing only a cotton blouse and slacks.

They went for the most part in silence. For one thing, it was quite hard work scrambling over the bare rock and for another it hardly seemed the right background for light conversation. Once or twice they stopped while her companion pointed out a seabird or a particularly beautiful ice floe, its pale green turned to gold by the sun, creaking and cracking as it went on its way south, but for the greater part of the time he went steadily ahead, turning to give her a hand over a particularly tricky bit.

They were cutting across a curve in the coastline, somewhere Annis hadn't been yet, for on her boat trips they almost always went in the other direction. Now they rounded the last massive cliff and she caught her breath.

The mountains stretched in front of them, sweeping down to the sea, their snow-capped tops contrasting with the dark grey of their slopes and the dark blue of the sea. Their line was broken directly before them, though, and a fjord, its beginnings lost in a great glacier a mile or more away, cut them in two. Its water was smooth and still and dark, for the mountains held back the sun, and the barren shore, thick with ice, looked grandly desolate. It seemed incredible to Annis that anything should want to live there, but the doctor had been right. The seals were packed snugly side by side along the side of the fjord, with the giant male seals sitting on ice floes, guarding them. They looked fatherly and a little pompous, but they never took their eyes away from the mother seals and their pups.

'We can get closer, they're not afraid of us,' said the doctor quietly, and helped her across a ridge of rock.

'How can anyone bear to kill them?' demanded Annis fiercely. 'Look, their eyes are just like ours and the babies look just like our babies.'

Her companion's firm mouth twitched slightly but he answered her gravely: 'Indeed they do, and I deplore their killing, but here they seem safe, although one wonders how they can live so contentedly in this barren land.'

'Yes, but it's beautiful too, although it frightens me. I had no idea—I don't know what I expected, but I felt sick with fright when I got here. It's not like anything else ...' She felt she wasn't explaining very well, but he seemed to understand her.

'It's still our world,' he reminded her. 'It's hard to equate it with Piccadilly Circus or the Dam Square in Amsterdam, but it's utter peace and quiet and awe-inspiring nature at her most magnificent.'

She was surprised into saying: 'Oh, do you feel like that about it, too? Only I couldn't have put it as well as you have.'

She took a careless step and slipped and his hand grasped her arm, and then without any hesitation at all, he caught her close and kissed her. It wasn't at all the kind of kiss Arthur had been in the habit of giving her; he took his time over it and she thought confusedly that she was enjoying it very much.

His pleasantly friendly: 'You're such a beautiful girl, Annis—that and the midnight sun's magic ...'

brought her back with a sickening bump to a prosaic world again. Commendably, she managed to say coolly:

'It is magic, isn't it, and I wouldn't have missed it for all the world. I'd like to come here in winter, though ...'

He had thrown a great arm round her shoulders and she felt a thrill of pleasure.

'Would you indeed?' He turned his head to study her face. 'Yes, I do believe you mean that. I came up here a couple of years ago for a few weeks and it's quite extraordinary, more so because the people who live here take it for granted.'

'But you live in Holland?' She had never asked him any questions before; probably he would snub her politely, but he didn't.

'Oh, yes—I've a practice in a small country town; Goes—it's near Middelburg, if you know where that is.'

'Well, of course I do,' she protested indignantly, 'though I've never been to Holland.'

She felt a strong urge to ask him if he were married, if he had children and a family. She wanted to know more about him, but although he had kissed her with some warmth, his manner was as casual as it always had been and she was sensible enough to know that kissing a girl when there wasn't another female to be seen for miles was a perfectly normal thing for a man to do. She stifled a sigh and asked: 'What exactly does everyone do here? Freddy doesn't make it very clear.'

He threw her a quick look. 'It's a radio station, you knew that? We send weather reports and relay shipping news and there's an early warning system ...'

'Oh, I see ... I suppose I'm not supposed to be too curious?'

'The boss relies on your discretion, but unless you happened to be an electronics expert with a very inquisitive nose, I don't think you would be any the wiser.'

'Well, I'm not particularly interested,' she said loftily, and he laughed. 'You're not bored?'

'Bored? Heavens, no—how could I possibly be that? I don't have much time for a start, do I? and there's such a lot to cram into each day.'

'And there's a treat in store for you in a couple of days. Fetching the stores from Ny Aalesund. There's one shop there and it stocks everything, although not all of it is on sale to the tourists from the cruising trips coming from Norway during the summer. The men will give you a list as long as your arm and you'd better make one for yourself. We only go once a month.'

'Don't you go on the Coastal Express?'

'Sometimes, but the jetty isn't any good and we have to go out to her by boat, and transferring the stuff from her on the return journey is quite a lengthy business.'

'Then how do we go?' Annis gazed round her. 'There's no road ...'

'We fly.'

'Oh—does the plane come from Tromso?'

'No—there's one here, it's in a boathouse on the other side of the radio station. I don't suppose you've been as far.'

She shook her head. 'No. It'll be fun to go to Ny Aalesund.'

They went back presently and she went to the hut and joined Freddy, writing one of his rare, sketchy letters. He looked up when she went in. 'Hullo—enjoy the seals?'

'Enormously.'

'Jake's a good fellow to be with, never gets worked up about anything. I'm told that he's much sought after by the birds.'

'Don't be vulgar, Freddy.' She added carelessly: 'He's not so young, though, is he?'

Freddy grinned. 'Thirty-five, very up-and-coming in his profession, too. A worthy target for your charms, love.'

She turned a wintry eye on him. 'Freddy, I've already begged you not be be vulgar. I'm sure Doctor van Germert is a very pleasant man, that's all.'

He sighed loudly. 'Don't tell me that you're pining for that dreary Arthur?'

Annis giggled. 'Don't be ridiculous! That's why I came here—we weren't getting anywhere and I'd discovered that I couldn't possibly marry him.'

'Bully for you, ducky. I found him a drip, not your sort.'

'What's my sort?' She had sat down on a folding chair and had picked up the map she had been studying each day in the hope that she would know exactly where she was.

'Jake.'

She put the map down carefully. Her voice was light and a little amused. 'I'm waiting for a real charmer, Freddy—I'd like to be swept off my feet.'

Freddy turned back to his writing. 'As long as you

find them again,' he warned her.

It was at breakfast the next day that someone asked: 'Who's going with you, Jake?'

'Annis.' The doctor didn't even look at her as he spoke. 'Have your lists ready by this evening, will you? We'll leave early.'

'And what is early?' asked Annis sweetly. 'I don't seem to have been told much about this ...'

He refused to be ruffled. 'After the night shift's breakfast,' he told her blandly. 'The second breakfast men can manage for themselves—we'll be back in time for you to cook supper.'

She eyed him frostily. So she was to cook supper, was she, after a hectic day shopping in a strange language among strange people, not to mention the trip there and back. She only hoped whoever was to fly the plane was a nice levelheaded man who didn't expect her to get thrilled every time they hit a pocket of air and dropped like a stone ...

'Will you have time to show Annis the hospital, Jake?' asked someone.

'I thought it might be an idea; I've a job or two to do there, anyway.'

Annis's interest quickened. It would be fun to see a hospital so far from the rest of the world, and she began to wonder about it, not listening to the talk around her.

She would have liked to have worn something more feminine than slacks and a shirt on this, the highlight of her stay, but common sense warned her that the weather might change with a speed she hadn't quite got used to, and probably the ground was rock. She wore sensible shoes, her new pale blue slacks and a white cotton blouse with a blue and white striped sweater to pull over it, and covered it with an apron while she saw to breakfast.

She studied the lists she had been given while she ate her breakfast through a chorus of items which had been forgotten. She already had a list of food and necessities and how she was going to get the lot in a day was beyond her, although with only one shop it might be easier. She finished her meal and only then noticed that the doctor wasn't there. Perhaps she was late— she got to her feet in a panic, gathering her plates and cup and saucer together. 'I should go,' she cried to those around her. 'Who's flying the plane?'

'I am,' said Jake, coming in through the door with maddening slowness. 'And I haven't had my breakfast yet, so don't panic.'

'I am not panicking,' declared Annis crossly. She added: 'Can you fly a plane, then?'

There was a chorus of kindly laughter. 'It's his plane, Annis,' she was told. 'He's really very good at it, too, you don't have to be nervous.'

'I'm not in the least nervous.' She shot a glance at the doctor, calmly eating his breakfast, taking so little notice of anyone that he might have been at his own table, quite alone. Not alone, she decided, her thoughts taking off as usual; he'd have a dog—perhaps two ...

'Have you a dog?' she asked suddenly, and everyone looked bewildered. All except the doctor, who looked up, studied her face carefully and answered, just as though he had read her thoughts: 'Yes. He sits with me while I eat my breakfast. If you like to collect your.

purse or whatever, I'll be with you in a couple of minutes.'

The plane was moored to the jetty, a small seaplane, very spick and span, bouncing up and down in what Annis considered to be a quite unnecessarily boisterous manner.

'It's the wind catching her,' explained the doctor, just as though Annis had spoken out loud. 'Jump in.'

'Isn't there anyone else coming?'

He shook his head. 'No.' And because he obviously wasn't going to say more than that, she climbed aboard and settled herself down.

She hadn't expected to enjoy the trip because she had to confess to a secret fear that the small craft might drop like a stone on to the white wastes below them, or lose a wing or a vital bit of its engine, but presently her fears left her, probably because her companion exhibited much the same sort of calm as a bus driver going along a well-remembered country lane.

After a little while he began to point out various landmarks. 'There's Magdalena Bay straight ahead, and Konigsfjord is round the corner. The cruisers all go there and then on up to the ice barrier.'

They had been following the coastline for a good deal of the time, now he banked and pointed downwards. 'There's Ny Aalesund; we'll come down by the pier—it's quite a walk to the shop and the road's a mixture of coal and lava. We'll take a taxi if you would rather.'

'A taxi? Here? Surely they can't earn their living? Where are the roads?'

'There are two, and they don't go far, but all the

same a car can be useful to get about. In the winter everyone has snow scooters.'

He came down some way from the shore and taxied slowly up to the pier, where several men appeared to make the plane fast. 'Out you get,' said the doctor. 'We'll go straight to the shop, though I suggest that we stop at the post office and have coffee.'

Annis could see no post office, no houses, for that matter, just a dusty track alongside a bridge being built over a rambling little river hurrying down to the sea. The track opened out on to a road once they had crossed the bridge and she could see it winding uphill, past some wooden houses. The doctor took her arm. 'It's much nicer once we get to the top,' he said reassuringly.

CHAPTER THREE

JAKE was right. They gained the top of the slope and found grass round its curve—rough, tough very short grass, it was true, but a welcome green. The tiny town before them stretched back from the sea, its houses built on either side of the tumbling, untidy little torrent they had already crossed further back, its origins lost in the massive glacier at the head of the valley, some miles away. Mountains towered in a great curve, their sides scarred by mine workings. The houses were wooden, as was the white-painted church, and on the far side of the stream there was a group of new houses, so modern and sedate they might have been in a London suburb instead of at the back of beyond.

The doctor had given Annis time to stand and stare, now he suggested that they should start their walk. 'Though you can ride if you wish,' he reminded her, 'but there's plenty to see.'

The houses were at first rather old-fashioned and weather-worn, but by the time they had reached the church they looked more modern and well-kept, and the church itself, with its own little house attached to it, was pristine against the dull rock of the mountains behind it. There was lichen beside the cinder road, and tiny flowers and a few patches of the same coarse grass, and there were people too. Annis was surprised to see two young women wheeling babies in prams, and the doctor laughed at her astonished face. 'People have babies everywhere in the world,' he observed. 'The hospital here is more than adequate to deal with any kind of surgery; there are a doctor and a surgeon, mid-wives, nurses—you name it, they've got it.'

They passed a lonely little graveyard half way up the lower slopes of the mountains and Annis said soberly: 'I suppose they must love being here—I mean, to live here all their lives and die here too.'

'I think they're very content and happy, and the children look beautiful—there's a good school and they go to Norway for their higher education and come home for holidays. There's a film evening, too, and dancing each week, and a library.'

The road forked presently, the fork crossing the stream and climbing along its other bank. 'There's the hospital,' said Jake, 'that long building built up from the road. We'll keep straight on, though. The post office is at the end, you can see it now, then we cross a bridge and the shop's on the other side.'

'Where does the road go to?'

'It doesn't. There are a few houses beyond the shop, and it stops there; there's no way through the moun-tains.'

It was a clear morning now, although every now and then the mountains disappeared in cloud, and it was warm walking. Annis was glad when they stopped presently and had their coffee, but she wasn't allowed to linger. 'I'm due at the hospital in half an hour; I'll take you to the shop and leave you there and pick you up later.'

She looked at him in horror. 'But you can't—I won't

understand a word they say . . .'

He chuckled. 'Don't worry, they'll understand you and speak English, too.'

The shop, when they reached it, didn't look like a shop at all. There was no display window, only a side door opening out into a large hall, filled with counters displaying everything one could think of. Jake, having introduced her to the manager, took himself off, saying he would be back in two hours, and she was left to roam round with her list. Toothpaste, shaving soap, socks, sweets, notepaper and picture post cards; she collected them all and then went upstairs, where the tourists didn't go, and bought her stores. And even then she had a little time to spare, so leaving the obliging manager to pack everything up and send it down to the plane, she went back to examine the trinket counter. There were some pretty things there; she was examining a silver bracelet decorated with blue enamel leaves which had taken her fancy when Jake loomed up silently beside her.

'Ready?' he wanted to know, and then: 'Are you buying that?'

She laid it down with reluctance. 'Not now—perhaps if I come again . . .' She looked up at him. 'Are we going back? I thought you would be here all day.'

'So I am, but I need my strength kept up like anyone else. I usually eat at the hospital, but the pastor's invited us both to lunch. I borrowed a jeep from the hospital, so you won't need to walk.' He led the way ouside. 'Did you get everything?'

'Yes, it's being sent down to the plane. What do you do at the hospital?'

'Give the anaesthetics—fill in for whichever of the two wants a day off. I like to keep my hand in; there's not enough to do at the station.'

'Have you a large practice in Goes?'

He shot the jeep down the road and over the bridge. 'So-so.'

Annis sighed; it was a pity he never talked about himself. She made a sedate remark about the weather and wondered why he smiled. She could have asked him that too, she supposed, and probably had no reply.

The pastor's house was delightful; simply furnished but so comfortable that Annis could imagine that living there, even through the long dark winter, would be a pleasure. The pastor was a young man with a pretty, sturdy wife and three small boys, and she envied Jake's knowledge of Norwegian, although they spoke English to her and the other girl lost no time in drawing her on one side to ask questions about clothes and what was fashionable.

They sat down to lunch almost immediately because Jake had to be back in the hospital within the hour; poached salmon and jacket potatoes and Lucullus cake and great cups of coffee. Annis was glad of the coffee; she had been invited to sample the Aqua Vitae and her head hadn't felt quite right since.

Jake went shortly, and she felt a pang of disappointment that he hadn't asked her if she would like to see over the hospital—indeed, she had felt sure he would, but he had gone with nothing more than a casual warning to be down at the plane by four o'clock. So she spent the afternoon with her new friends, and refusing their kind offers to walk down with her, left in good time. She had enjoyed her afternoon. She had been into the church, and most of her questions about the town and its inhabitants had been answered. All the same, she felt lingering regret at not seeing the hospital: after all, she was a nurse ...

Jake overtook her half way there, driving the jeep and with a young man beside him, presumably to drive it back again. 'Kai Dohlen,' introduced Jake, 'he's the surgeon.' He stuffed her between them and raced on down to the tiny harbour where they spent a few minutes talking before getting into the plane. As he taxied away across the water, Jake said: 'Nice fellow, Kai. Sverre, the physician, is even nicer.'

'It was nice meeting one of them, at least,' observed Annis tartly.

'Sore at me because I didn't take you sightseeing at the hospital? I've been busy, there was a lot to do today and it would have meant a nurse staying on duty to show you round. Next time, I hope.'

'Perhaps.' She had her eyes shut, just while they took off, and it was annoying to be told that she might open them again, especially as he was laughing.

'I'm only a little nervous,' she explained haughtily. 'The mountains look rather too close ...'

His black brows rose. 'Close? I find them magnificent.'

'Well, so do I, but a bit overpowering. I'm not sure if I like mountains after all, especially when they're at the top of the world.' She stared out at the grim coastline. 'I—I wanted to get away from hospital for a while ...'

'Ah—a love affair gone wrong.' He sounded faintly

mocking and she fired up immediately.

'Nothing of the sort, it was just—just that I didn't want to get married—not to him anyway.'

'Let me guess. Shorter than you—you're a big girl, aren't you, Annis—very worthy, no sense of humour, good at his job and saves his money.'

Annis choked. 'You have no right . . .'

'None at all, that's why . . .' he broke off. 'There's something down there—I'm going lower to have a look.'

It was a small motorboat, dangerously close to the rocks and drifting nearer to them at every second.

'What will you do?' cried Annis breathlessly.

'Pick him up.' The doctor sounded laconic, as though picking up people out of the sea was a daily occurrence.

The mountains looked more terrifying than ever now because Jake was flying so close to them, but Annis forgot her fear as she watched the figure in the boat waving frantically, although it all came back, half choking her as Jake brought the plane down several hundred yards from the boat and taxied towards it; the sea looked so dark and cold and the grey masses, with their remote snow-covered peaks, seemed to be closing in on them.

'Get away from the door,' advised Jake, 'and go to the back; sit on the stores if you must. I shall have to take off again as soon as I can, so be ready to give first aid if you have to.'

His calm quieted her squeaking nerves and she did as he bade her, watching while he opened the door, sidling close to the boat and its occupant. He shouted something presently and a moment later a young man clambered clumsily into the plane. Jake leaned across him and shut the door and began to taxi away from the shore, and Annis, mindful of instructions, moved cautiously forward again. The man was wet and shivering but didn't appear to be hurt. He grinned at her as she offered him a blanket and said: 'To be rescued by an angel—I am indeed fortunate.'

Annis was rummaging round for something to use as a towel. 'I didn't rescue you,' she pointed out matter-of-factly, 'Doctor van Germert did.'

'From the station?' He glanced at the doctor. 'Of course I have heard of you. I'm the replacement for Hagmann—Ola Julsen—I have also heard of the English nurse.'

The doctor nodded and said something in Norwegian and Julsen answered him. It gave Annis a moment in which to study the two men. The Norwegian wasn't as big as the doctor, but he had blond good looks and fair curling hair and the brightest blue eyes she had ever seen. He looked romantic, even though he was soaking wet, and she was a romantic girl. She stole a look at Jake; he was good-looking too in a dark heavy way, a little forbidding too and overpoweringly large, and his eyes were dark, sometimes they looked black. He was treating the whole episode with a matter-of-factness which was the exact opposite of the romantic. She could easily imagine their unexpected companion remembering anniversaries with dozens of red roses; the doctor would most likely never give them a thought ... He made matters even more prosaic now by saying: 'Take those wet things off—

there's the blanket Annis gave you—don't mind her, she's a nurse, as you know.'

She bristled at his careless tone; she could have been a middle-aged matron in a starched apron. She looked up and caught the Norwegian's merry eye and smiled involuntarily.

They hadn't far to go now and once wrapped in his blanket the Norwegian regaled them with lighthearted talk, speaking an almost perfect English, smiling at Annis from time to time, a secret smile which gave her the pleasant feeling of sharing a joke with him.

Jake took the plane down neatly and once the first little bustle of their return had been done with told her to take Julsen over to the surgery. 'I'll be along in a minute,' he told her. 'I'd better have a look at him before he goes to his hut.'

Annis was surprised to find that she felt a little shy of her patient; perhaps it was the way he looked at her—half laughing as though he could read her thoughts and sense her excitement at meeting him. She opened up the surgery, found a dressing gown for him and went to put on her white gown, and by the time she had done that the doctor had joined them. But she need not have bothered with the gown, for he told her composedly that he wouldn't need her. 'Perhaps you could see to the stores,' he suggested blandly, and held the door open for her before shutting it firmly behind her.

Annis, a little put out, went back to the main hut and dealt with the provisions, handed out the things she had bought for the men, ticked off her list with the boss and then sped away to get the evening meal. The men had done all the hard work, it was only left to her to cook it. She did so in a rather absentminded manner, her thoughts centred on the new arrival.

He came to supper presently and found a seat opposite her, so that every time she looked up it was to find his eyes upon her. She found it disconcerting but nicely disturbing too. Life at the station was pleasant enough, but there had been no hint of romance. She was on excellent terms with all the men, just as she was on excellent terms with Freddy, but somehow Ola Julsen was different.

And within the next few days she discovered how different. He went on and off duty just the same as everyone else, but somehow he was always free when she was and if he wasn't, she would find something left for her in the sitting room of her hut; a fossil, a sea-bird's feather, a book of poetry with marked passages, so that he was never far from her thoughts. And when they were both free at the same time, they walked along the narrow strip of flat rocky ground by the station, or sat watching the ever-changing sea, and once or twice he took her out in one of the boats. They talked a great deal, at least Ola did most of the talking; Annis was content to sit and listen to him describing Norway and its beauties. He seemed to know the entire country very well, but when she asked him where he lived, he made some evasive answer, nor did he tell her much about himself. He had parents and a brother, he had been to university and taken an honours degree, he was determined to make a name for himself in the world of electronics ...

He asked her a great deal about her own life,

though, wanting to know, half laughing, if she had plans to marry, what she intended to do when she left Spitzbergen, and she answered all his questions quite honestly because it didn't occur to her to do otherwise. She knew that she was happy, Ola was so different from Arthur.

But she didn't let her romance interfere with her work. She worked, in fact, a good deal harder, feeling guilty that she should be so content with her simple life, and after his first few attempts to talk to her about it, Freddy had given up his halfhearted advice. She had looked at him in surprise when he had first broached the subject of her spending so much of her time with Ola. 'But only when I'm free to do so,' she pointed out reasonably. 'He's good company.' And when he had tried again a day or two later: 'Don't you like him, Freddy?'

'No,' said Freddy, 'and don't ask me why, because I don't know.'

'In that case it's nonsense to object to me seeing him.' She added impatiently: 'We're not sly about it, you know, anyone can see us—heaven knows there's nowhere to hide round here.' She had laughed at him and Freddy had smiled reluctantly.

The only other person to say anything to her was Jake, and he merely remarked in the most casual of voices that it had been a lucky day when Ola had joined them. 'Nice for you,' he had continued placidly, 'he's a good talker.'

She had murmured a reply and applied herself to the old-fashioned Thomas's splint she was padding.

It was ten days or so after their expedition to Ny

Aalesund that she and Ola walked along the treacherous shoreline in order to get a better view of some seabirds she hadn't seen before. They were some distance from the station but still within sight of it when Annis noticed the doctor perched on the rocks some yards ahead of them, his binoculars to his eyes. At the same time there was a shout behind them and one of the men, a young Finn, came running towards them. 'He's coming too fast,' said Annis. 'If he slips he'll fall into the sea.'

The words were hardly out of her mouth before the boy stumbled, rolled over and slid with a sickening splash into the icy water. 'He's concussed, he'll drown —Ola, help him!'

The Norwegian hadn't moved, he still didn't move when Jake passed him, kicked off his heavy boots and slid into the water. It was Annis who stumbled over the rocks, took precarious hold of one of them, ready to do what she could when Jake surfaced. It seemed a lifetime before he reappeared, the unconscious boy with him. Annis leaned nearer and then paused to shout over her shoulder. 'Don't just stand there, Ola, go for help—a stretcher and four men at least—and hurry!'

She turned back to where Jake's head showed above the dark water. 'What shall I do?' she asked him urgently, and was shocked at his white face. 'Jake?' she called again, terrified that he was going to drown before help reached them.

He had edged nearer, treading water. 'My God, it's cold. Here, have you got a good hold on that rock? Then catch hold of anything you can reach—his overalls are tough, get a grip on them.'

She clutched a fold of heavy wet cloth so that she took a little of the boy's weight, not much but perhaps it helped Jake; she hoped so, because she didn't think that she would be able to stay as she was for more than a few more minutes. She was shaking with fright, too, and icy cold, her chattering teeth clattering away in her head so that she was barely aware of running feet and then the cautious approach of half a dozen men. One of them pulled her gently back while two more leaned down and dragged the unconscious boy on to the rocks and she cried idiotically: 'Oh, get Jake out—he'll drown!' But there was no need for her to say anything, three men were hauling on him already, breathing heavily and grunting with the effort as they tried to get a hold on him. She stared at him. He looked strange and he hadn't uttered a word; not until they were on the point of dragging him out too did she hear him say in a tight voice: 'Go easy, will you? I've busted my leg.'

Her teeth didn't chatter any more, she forgot that she was shivering with cold. The men with the stretcher were waiting beside her. She turned to the nearest and said calmly: 'Go to the surgery, bring the splints behind the door and the straps, scissors and one of the sterile packs on the top of the cupboard.' She barely watched him go before saying urgently: 'Will you try and get two men on each leg as you lift him; get him straight on to the stretcher—it's going to be difficult ...'

It was; by the time they had done it the man was back with the splints. She knelt down beside Jake and took a huge icy hand in hers. 'Which leg, Jake?'

'The left—just below the knee.' He smiled very faintly at her and then spoke to one of the men. 'Paul, get something warm for Annis to put on and bring some Aqua Vitae, we all need a nip.'

She wasn't listening; she was snipping his trouser seams with numb hands, anxious to see what the damage was. It was vital to get him indoors as soon as possible, but it was equally vital that she should see just how bad a fracture he had. Bad enough, but it could have been worse; both bones were broken, their jagged ends just showing through the wound below his knee; she didn't dare to bring them into alignment, all she could do was to lay a sterile dressing over the area of fracture and bandage it lightly. And while she was doing it someone came to drape a thick sweater round her shoulders and offer her a drink of Aqua Vitae; its fiery taste took her breath and made her eyes water, but it warmed her too. Jake was given a long drink too and she asked: 'Do you feel anything, Jake?'

'Not a thing, now. It's a compound, isn't it?'

'Yes—we'll take you to hospital at once. Harald must go too.'

One of the men turned to look at her. 'How come you stayed here? Why didn't Ola send you? He should have—dangerous it was, leaving you here ...'

Annis didn't speak; the same ugly thought had been at the back of her mind ever since Ola had turned and run back to the station and left her. It was the doctor who said: 'I daresay he thought Annis might slip on the rocks—and that would have been a disaster.' He added something in Norwegian and was answered by gruntling replies, and then she was finished; the splint neatly tied and Jake ready to be carried back to the station.

Once in the surgery she kept two of the men with her to help and while they were stripping Jake of his wet clothes, answered the boss's questions. There weren't many of them; she made short work of them and asked: 'The plane—can Jake be taken at once? It's a nasty fracture, it needs an expert to set it.'

'They're getting it ready now—you'll go with them both, Annis. We'll manage for a day or two. Stay there and do what you can to help and send a message from the hospital—they'll radio us if you ask them. Is there anything you can't leave?'

She thought. 'No. There's Max's hand—it'll need dressing each day, but the stitches aren't due out for another three days, and there's Eding's bruised leg ... Nils'—Nils was the first aid man—'can cope with them.'

'Good—get some dry clothes on and something warm and pack a few things. I'll have a word with Jake. Is he in pain?'

'No, I don't think so, but he will be as soon as he's warmer. I'll get him to write himself up for something so that I can give it at once. Have you radioed the hospital?'

The boss smiled gently. 'Ten minutes ago.' He patted her arm. 'Run along.'

Thinking about it afterwards, Annis couldn't remember much about the flight. Harald regained consciousness before they started, and Jake, who had remained stubbornly aware of what was going on all around him, even to the giving of advice as to what should be done about his leg and Harald's head, had to submit to her coaxing presently and allow her to give him a pain-killing injection.

An ambulance had been waiting for them and men to help in the difficult task of getting the two men off the plane and into it, and they were ready and waiting for them when they had reached the hospital. Harald had been X-rayed and put to bed under observation, and Jake had been taken straight to theatre and his leg examined before he too went to X-ray.

'An untidy fracture,' she had been told. 'It will be necessary to give a general anaesthetic, but there is no reason to suppose that it will be troublesome; we will reduce the facture and put the leg in plaster and leave a window over the wound.' The surgeon had smiled at her kindly. 'I am to understand that you will remain for a few days? That will be of great help to us. If you could look after your two patients? You will be relieved, of course, and there will not be a great deal to do ...' His nice grey eyes twinkled suddenly. 'I think that Jake will wish to do everything for himself.'

'Well, he's not going to,' Annis had said, and had had to eat her words a dozen times since, after only a day, she was only too aware that Jake was a bad patient; he never complained and up to a point did exactly what he was told to do, but he insisted on washing himself and only a firm hand on his huge chest had restrained him from getting out of bed the moment the plaster on his leg was dry.

'You'll stay where you are, Doctor,' said Annis crisply. 'You'll get up all in good time, in the meantime you'll oblige me by wriggling your toes as frequently as possible.'

He had laughed then. 'My dear Annis, I'll do anything to oblige you.'

She was on her way to the door to give Harald a blanket bath. 'Yes, I know, but only when it suits you.'

He was up the next day, sitting in a big chair by the window, looking down on to the stream below, declaring that he was perfectly able to go back to the station, and was only dissuaded by his colleagues by pointing out that he would have to have another X-ray in a day or two and finish his antibiotics as well as being certain that the small wound above the break was completely free from infection. Besides, Harald needed another day or two's rest before he could be moved; his concussion had proved light, but he still complained of headache. So after the first couple of days Annis found herself with little to do; the doctor was friendly and now that he had arranged things to suit himself, a model patient, but he showed no desire to have more of her company than her professional duties warranted and there was not much more to do for Harald. She gave a hand in the wards, struggling with a word or two of Norwegian while she made beds and undertook routine tasks which she supposed were the same in hospitals all over the world.

It was on the fourth afternoon, finding herself free for a couple of hours, that she was wondering what to do with them, when one of the nurses who spoke a little English came to tell her that there was someone to see her.

It would be Ola, she thought excitedly, frantically

brushing her hair and doing her face. Thank heaven she had already changed into slacks and a shirt ...

He was waiting outside and came to meet her with a charming smile. 'Annis, my dear—you see that I have come to see you. I travelled on the Coastal Express and this evening I fly out again.'

She was breathless at the sight of him. 'Oh, is there a plane going back to the station? We're not going for another day or two.' She smiled widely at him. 'Oh, Ola, it's so nice to see you again.'

'And I find it more than nice to see you.' He took her arm. 'We will take a little walk, it is pretty if we go past the shop. There are a few trees and one can pretend that we are far from this desolate land.'

'Well, you know, I don't find it so very desolate, but I have got an hour to spare ...'

'An hour is so short a time.' He squeezed her arm against him. 'And I have much to say. It has been very pleasant meeting you, Annis. You are such a lovely girl and we have had so much time together. I shall miss you.'

They were climbing the dusty road past the shop and although the sun was shining, Annis felt cold. 'You're going away?'

He gave the little rumble of laughter which she had found so charming. 'But of course; I came only for a few weeks, I must return to Norway.'

'Oh, to your work ...'

'Yes, and to my wife.'

The cold spread over the whole of her. 'I didn't know you were married; you didn't tell me.'

'Of course not, if I had done so you would have

ignored me, would you not, Annis? Even though you were so greatly attracted to me—you are, I think, that kind of a girl; it is not, how do you say, cricket, to allow another girl's husband to get too attentive.' He laughed down at her. 'And you would not have kissed me so very warmly, would you?'

Annis stopped and took her arm away from his hold. 'It's time I got back,' she said steadily. 'No, I don't suppose I would, and since you mention cricket, I don't think you know the rules very well yourself, do you, Ola?'

She spoke in a calm little voice which gave away none of her raging feelings. Humiliation, and anger and a hopeless sorrow were jumbled up inside her, and the sorrow was winning fast. At any moment she might burst into tears, something she was determined not to do at any cost. She walked a little faster. 'How long will it take you to fly back?' she asked politely.

He looked surprised and relieved but not the least ashamed of himself, which helped her enormously not to cry. She kept the conversation determinedly upon nothing much in particular until they reached the hospital, when she looked at her watch again, declared that she was late, and left him before he could say so much as goodbye.

She still had half an hour before she was on duty. She made her way through the building and along the corridor which led to the small wing where the nurses lived, almost running in her effort to get to her room and have a good howl. She was passing the doctor's room when he called her and she instinctively went in; he was her patient and anything could have happened.

He was still sitting by the window, looking like a thundercloud.

'What is Julsen doing here?' he demanded. 'And what exactly ...' he stopped, examined her face for a long moment and said quite gently: 'No, it doesn't matter, Annis.' He picked up some papers, not looking at her now. 'Don't hurry back on duty—there's nothing for you to do for an hour or so.'

CHAPTER FOUR

ANNIS took no notice of Jake's advice. She cried herself to a wet and soggy stop, had a shower, changed into her uniform overall and put on a pair of dark glasses. Then she went on duty at the time expected of her; even if her heart was broken she still had a job to do.

She went first to Harald, fast becoming his normal self, and then to Jake to give him his final antibiotic jab.

He barely glanced up from his book as she went in to his room and his 'Hullo' was brief. It wasn't until she was rubbing the place she had injected that he put up a deliberate hand and removed her dark glasses.

She glared at him from puffed-up eyes. 'Give those back!' she snapped, and then had the wind taken out of her sails by his instant compliance. He didn't say anything either, only asked her to get the male orderly to go to his room when he had the time and went back to his reading.

He put the book down the moment she had left the room, however, and when the orderly arrived, wrote busily for a few moments and then handed him what he had written with the request that it might be handed in to the radio room as soon as possible.

It wasn't until the following morning, while Annis was peering at the fast healing wound, neatly surrounded by plaster, that Jake remarked casually: 'We're going back to the station today—Willy sent a message.'

She put down her forceps carefully. 'You're not fit to go. Oh, I know you whip around on your crutches, but you've only just finished your antibiotics.'

His black eyes gleamed with amusement. 'My dear Annis, it's only my leg which is out of action, not me. I can manage perfectly—the men can come to me, and if I need to move around you can drive me in the jeep.'

'Indeed I'll do no such thing.' Her splendid bosom heaved with annoyance. How like him to arrange everything just so to please himself!

'Oh, I thought you could drive ...'

'Of course I can drive.'

'Well, what's the argument, then? Not scared?'

'No, I am not.' She added accusingly: 'I suppose you arranged all this behind my back.'

His dark eyes held no expression. 'Yes; it's time we were all back at work. I'm bored stiff and so is Harald, and you're unhappy.'

Annis blushed. 'I don't see,' she began stiffly, 'that you need to poke your nose into my business.'

'But my darling girl, I have done no such thing; for one thing I've much too much to do that's far more interesting. What gave you the idea, I wonder?'

The blush, which had subsided, got worse. 'You're impossible,' she told him coldly, and went away to help make the beds in the general ward.

But she realised that sooner or later she would have to find out at what time they were to go. When she had finished her work in the ward, she went back again to

Jake's room. 'When are we going?' she wanted to know.

He was standing balancing himself on his crutches by the window, looking out at the world outside. 'After lunch—two o'clock at the latest. The weather report isn't good, so we won't hang around.' He glanced at her. 'If you would pack our bits and pieces?'

She went to see Harald next, still a little pale but playing cards with another patient. 'We're going back after lunch,' she told him. 'I'll pack your things—do you want to say goodbye to anyone? I should do it before lunchtime, Jake says he wants to get away on time.'

She went away to pack her own scanty possessions, say goodbye to her colleagues and new-found friends and then to help serve lunches. She had barely time to eat her own when she was warned to be ready to go within a few minutes and went back to Jake's room to find him lying back in his chair, asleep.

She frowned. She hadn't been told how they were to get down to the plane—Harald had said carelessly: 'Oh, with the jeep, of course,' and the fear that she might be expected to drive the thing had been simmering in her head ever since. She turned to go and find someone to settle the vexed question, but Jake stopped her. Without opening his eyes he said: 'They'll drive us down. There'll be an orderly with us to help me on board; all you need to do is stand about and look beautiful.'

She gave an indignant snort and he opened an eye. 'Do you blush when you're angry or because you're shy?' he wanted to know.

'Neither. It's very warm in here.' She turned away towards the window and stared out at the road—the road where she and Ola had walked only yesterday. The memory of it all washed over her in a great wave of misery and she stood there, fighting back a desire to have a good howl, even if Jake were to stand there mocking her.

But he didn't do anything of the sort. His voice was gentle. 'Don't try and creep back into yesterday,' he advised her, 'it never did any good. Come over here and I'll tell you who's off sick at the station ... nothing much, but as you'll have to take them in hand you'd better know.'

Annis forced herself to do as he asked so that despite herself she had no more time to think about Ola, and she was kept busy when the jeep arrived and even busier seeing Jake and Harald safely stowed in the plane. Freddy was piloting it and she was so occupied by all three of them asking questions and inviting her to express an opinion on every topic broached that she forgot all about herself.

They received a royal welcome, too. Anyone would think that we'd been away for years instead of a few days, thought Annis as she was borne away to give an account of herself and her patients to the boss. A quite unnecessary exercise as it turned out, for Jake was already there, sitting with his plastered leg stretched out on a stool, looking as though butter wouldn't melt in his mouth.

Willy gave her a thoughtful look over his old-fashioned spectacles.

'You look as though you could do with a few days off.'

Jake answered before she could even open her mouth. 'That's the last thing she needs; she's had several days tasting the delights of Ny Aalesund— daily visits to the shop, tea with the pastor, cards every evening with the nurses, not to mention all the bustle of hospital life. Besides, if she doesn't get down to the cooking stove pretty smartly, we shall have an unending queue of men with indigestion.'

Willy laughed, although his eyes were shrewd. 'I must say we missed your splendid meals.' He went on without giving Annis a chance to say if she wanted some free time, 'If you feel you can, we could all do with a good supper. If you like to start, my dear, I'll tell Jake about the few cuts and bruises which may need your attention.' He smiled dismissal and she went, not looking at Jake, tiresome man that he was, arranging everything to suit himself, as usual.

He certainly kept her busy during the next few days. No sooner had she finished one thing than he demanded something further of her, and as well as that he expected her to drive him each day to the radio station where some of his tests were being undertaken. She was speechless with annoyance the first time as well as being scared of going off the narrow track, but the doctor didn't appear to share her feelings; he sat beside her, his plastered leg sticking out awkwardly, carrying on a rambling chat about nothing much, and on the return journey he had his eyes shut, presenting the appearance of a man peacefully sleeping.

The fine weather held, but she didn't accept any of

the invitations to go out fishing with any of the men, or make expeditions to see the colonies of seals in the neighbourhood. Instead she sat in her room, thinking of Ola. He had treated her badly and she told herself unendingly that he wasn't worth another thought. Besides that, although she hadn't admitted it, even to herself, he had behaved very badly when Harald had fallen into the water. Even loving him as she did, she found that hard to forget. Why couldn't he have been like Jake, calm and resourceful and utterly dependable? And vexing too, she reminded herself, and then frowned fiercely because he had thumped on the door with his crutch and told her to come at once.

She had joined him reluctantly, but he had ignored that. 'There's a whale fairly close in to the shore,' he told her. 'We don't sight them very often, it's worth making an effort.'

Annis stopped herself just in time from asking him crossly what effort he was talking about and accompanied him down to the flat tongue of land where several men were standing, her heart in her mouth in case he should miss his footing and fall again. In the excitement of seeing her very first whale she forgot all about Ola.

It was strange to her that no one ever spoke of Ola; he had been with them for only a short time, but he had seemed popular with everyone. The wish to know as much as possible about him even though it was turning the knife in the wound caused her to ask Nils Vardal, a tough young Norwegian with an open face and a steady gaze, whose hand she was dressing: 'No one ever mentions Ola Julsen ...' She tried to sound casual.

He answered her instantly. 'Because we are ashamed of him. We are proud, we Norwegians, and I think brave. He left you in great danger with Jake—he should have remained with him and sent you for help. For this we do not forgive him easily.' He added as an afterthought: 'Also Jake said that we were not to speak of him to you.'

Annis bent her head over his hand. 'This is quite a nasty burn,' she managed to keep her voice calm. 'That was very considerate of him and all of you. You're all so nice—I love being here and I shall be sorry to go.'

'Not yet, surely? Freddy's staying until September. It'll be a bit wintry by then, of course.'

'I don't think I'd mind that—in fact I think I'd like it, but your regular nurse and cook will be coming back before then, won't she? I can't do her out of a job. Besides, I must find myself work in England again.'

'You wouldn't like to work in Norway?'

'I think I'd love it, but I can only speak about a dozen words. I shall go there on holiday though, just as soon as I can.' She straightened up. 'There, that should do, but come back tomorrow morning, will you? Jake will want to look at it.'

She tidied up slowly after Nils had gone, her thoughts busy. She had been a fool about Ola, but he had been so different from Arthur; she had really believed that he loved her too. Well, the quicker she got over it, the better, she told herself, at the same time acknowledging that it would need something rather out of the ordinary to make her do that.

And as it turned out, it was something out of the ordinary. It was three days later, after a period of lovely clear weather, that the grim mountain tops disappeared into heavy clouds and the sea, reflecting their grimness, took on an inky darkness. Willy warned her not to go far from the station: 'Just in case there's a bit of wind,' he advised her. 'We don't want you blown off your feet.'

She nodded obediently, privately of the opinion that nothing less than a team of wild horses would induce her to leave the shelter of the huts. It was something very different from wild horses which sent her down to the rocky shore, though. She had been standing at the surgery door, watching the sky grow even darker, when a gust of wind had blown a seabird against the rocks and it fell injured. Annis took another look at the sky; if she sprinted there and back she would be quite safe. There was little wind and only the beginnings of a faint, mistlike rain. She didn't even stop to get a jacket, but sped across the lichen-covered ground, across the tongue of rock and in the direction of the radio station. She could see the bird lying a few yards ahead, one wing flapping helplessly.

It made no objection to her picking it up; its wing was broken, but otherwise it seemed all right. She tucked it under her arm and began her return journey. She had reached the tongue of rock, the sea lashing it on both sides now, when she heard the wind, a soft, angry roar coming over the mountains, and a moment later it was upon her, rocking her on her feet and taking her breath. The bird fluttered helplessly and she grasped it tighter—she wasn't going to let it go now after having rescued it, all the same she had been foolish to disregard Willy's warning. The mist was swirling round her now, flung hither and thither by the wind. Annis wasn't a panicky girl, but now she would have liked to give way to panic. Instead she started forward again, terrified that she would be blown into the water or miss her way in the mist. She didn't see Jake at once, coming to meet her on his crutches, but when she did she caught her breath and then let it out in an urgent cry:

'Go back, Jake, do go back. You'll be blown over ... Jake!'

The last was really a very small scream, for the wind had caught her and turned her round and just for a moment she thought she would fall.

'I'm not sure if I was meant to go or come,' observed Jake in an ordinary voice which restored her calm a little. 'What are you doing here, anyway? I reminded Willy to tell you not to leave the station.'

She stood within the circle of one great arm, rather hampered by the crutches but feeling safe. 'He did. It was my fault—I saw this bird fall and I came to fetch it; I thought I'd be back long before anything happened.'

'Understandable but foolish.'

'I'm sorry, Jake. I didn't think. It's—it's rather frightening, isn't it?' She added: 'Only not now you're here.'

He made a small sound which might have been a laugh. 'Well, we'll have to stay for the moment; prob-

ably it won't last long and if it does, someone is bound
to come looking for us.'

She relaxed against his arm. 'You weren't looking
for me?' she asked uncertainly.

'Not exactly. I saw you running across towards the
radio station. How is that bird?'

'He's here, under my arm—I hope he's still alive.'
She was too squashed to see the creature. 'I can't really
see him, not without ... not unless you let go of me,
and I'm too scared for that.'

'I won't let you go.' His voice was placidly matter-
of-fact; there was nothing about it to set her heart
pounding and her suddenly chaotic thoughts racing,
so clear and so vivid that for an awful moment she
wondered if she had uttered them aloud. It wasn't Ola
she loved; he had become a cardboard figure meaning
nothing at all. Romantic he might have been, but
romance—that kind of romance didn't matter any
more, only Jake's enormous arm holding her safe and
his quiet, reassuring voice. She wanted to stay with him
for the rest of her life and there would never be anyone else; she knew that, even in the shock of her discovery, it stood out like a huge milestone and wasn't to
be denied. And at the same moment the whole glorious
wonder of it was doused by the knowledge that he
wasn't even faintly interested in her. He was kind and
friendly and careful of her, but in a casual, big-brother
fashion, and he had never bothered to spare her feelings ... and on top of that she wouldn't see him again
once she had left the station.

The quiet matter-of-fact voice brought her back to
reality. 'The mist's clearing, it usually does after a few

minutes, though it comes back sooner or later. We'll nip back now.' He took his arm away. 'Hold my crutch, and for God's sake look where you're putting your feet.' He glanced down briefly. 'You should be wearing your boots.'

Her meek: 'Yes, Jake,' was lost in the howling wind.

They reached her hut without mishap and he went in with her, to find Freddy taking his ease with a book. He looked up as they went in, said: 'Hullo, hardly the weather for a stroll, is it?' and went on reading.

His sister gave him a resigned look. 'We weren't strolling—there was this bird . . .'

She laid it gently on the table and Jake bent to examine it. 'A broken wing,' he pronounced, 'A wooden spatula should do—I'll get one from the surgery.'

Freddy got to his feet. 'I'll get it,' he said obligingly. 'You don't look quite so peaked, Sis, the tempest seems to have done you good.'

He wandered off and left the two of them, Annis standing nervously by the small centre table, aware that the doctor was studying her face.

'He's quite right,' he observed. 'You've quite lost your looks, Annis—perhaps you do need some days to yourself.'

She felt her cheeks redden; if he hadn't been handicapped with his crutches she would have thrown something at him. Unfair, of course, for she knew, none better, that the pale, serious face she was forced to look at each time she made it up was plain with its grief. And now it was another grief, not for Ola any more but for her companion's detached manner towards her. She could have burst into tears with the greatest of ease.

'Thank you, Doctor,' she told him austerely. 'I'm perfectly all right as I am, I certainly don't want days off; I know Ny Aalesund very well indeed now and there's plenty to keep me busy here.'

He grinned at her, lounging on his crutches. 'Well, I hardly thought you'd want to go back to Ny Aalesund, though I'm afraid you'll have to go once more before you leave to get the next lot of stores.' His eyes narrowed. 'Freddy will fly the plane—and take care not to rescue any handsome young men on the way.'

The fire died out of her cheeks, leaving them paper-white, and she had to bite her lip to stop from crying. She would never forgive herself if she did, and luckily Freddy came back then with the spatula.

'Nasty weather outside,' he remarked cheerfully, 'hope it wears itself out before morning, it's my early duty.'

Nobody answered him as he sat down again and picked up his book, and Jake moved to the table and began to splint the bird's wing. He had large hands, beautifully kept, and he was very gentle. When he had finished he looked across at Annis. 'Where shall we put him?'

She didn't quite look at him. 'There's that little empty room at the back; the window's covered in mesh —I'll put a tub of water there ... Food?'

'Fish. No difficulty there, you can get all you want; there's always someone fishing. It's a simple fracture, it shouldn't take long to knit. As soon as the weather clears we'll let him live outside. He won't go away; he can't fly and he'll have discovered that he's getting free meals.'

He gave her a lazy smile and went away and she listened anxiously to the tap of his crutches, terrified that he might fall.

Freddy said, without lifting his eyes from his book: 'Don't worry, Sis, he's able to look after himself.' And when she turned her green eyes on him: 'Nurses always fuss over their patients.' His look was limpid.

The bird proved a distraction which helped Annis. It was a suspicious creature, gobbling its fish while it eyed her suspiciously, trying to fly with its splinted wing held awkwardly, and after a couple of days, when the weather had cleared again and it was settled out of doors between the huts, it sat gloomily for the greater part of the day, but once it drew towards evening, even though it was never dark, it came to life, uttering piercing cries and waking everyone up. The doctor, taking a look at its wing after surgery, declared it to be a damned nuisance. 'We'll be handing out sleeping pills,' he complained to Annis. 'It's a good thing it's healing well.' He straightened up and leaned on a crutch. 'I've christened him Immortal.'

Annis frowned in thought. 'I can't quite see ...'

'Keats—there's a bit that goes: "The voice I hear this passing night ..."'

'Oh, I know: "Thou wast not born for death, Immortal bird."' She stroked the soft feathers of its head. 'He's rather a dear even though he's troublesome.'

'He longs to leave us.' Jake was sitting on the side of the table, peering at the little window in his plaster. 'Do you long to leave us, Annis?'

She had been managing very nicely during the last few difficult days; preserving a cool friendly manner, not allowing herself to cry in case he should make some remark about red eyes or lost looks, but sudden remarks like this one shook her. She didn't answer at once, indeed, she asked him instead if his leg were bothering him.

'No, not in the least,' he told her patiently. 'You haven't answered my question.'

'I've enjoyed being here,' she said at length, 'it's been quite an experience.' She stopped because she couldn't think of anything else to say.

'But not one you wish to repeat?' he asked softly.

'I really hadn't thought about it.' She frowned fiercely at him.

'And of course it's not my business, is it?' he observed easily. 'I shall be leaving in a couple of weeks' time.'

Annis caught her breath and then let it out carefully. She had always thought that she would go first, that she would see the last of him, standing with his crutches beside the other men, waving goodbye from the lonely little patch of civilisation, but it seemed that she was to be the one who was left behind. She drew another careful breath. 'You can't fly,' she pointed out.

'Why ever not? I don't need my feet, dear girl.'

'The doctors won't let you ...'

His thick eyebrows rose. 'I'm a doctor, Annis.'

His faintly mocking smile put an end to their conversation.

That evening, when Freddy came back to their hut, she wandered from her room in her dressing gown, her hairbrush in her hand.

'Had a good day?' she wanted to know.

'Fine—always do.' Freddy lowered himself into a chair. 'How come you're up so late? Is there any coffee?'

She had it ready. She fetched two mugs and sat down opposite him, and sipped in silence until he asked: 'What's up, Sis?'

She gave him a long look from her green eyes. 'Up? What should be up? There's nothing.' She added pettishly: 'And I do wish you wouldn't call me Sis.' And a moment later: 'I was wondering when I'm going.'

Freddy gave her a quick glance. 'Bored?'

'Heavens, no. But I do have to make a few plans, you know. Getting back to England and finding another job . . .'

'Well, why not ask Jake? He's going back in a couple of weeks—less. Sven's sister is almost due back, probably she'll arrive with Jake's replacement.' He put down his empty mug. 'I'm for bed, and you'd better go too or there'll be no breakfast for anyone in the morning. Ask Jake—he knows everything.'

All the same, Annis didn't take Freddy's advice for several days and by then the fortnight had dwindled to almost a week, but somehow the opportunity hadn't occurred, and now, taking the bull by the horns, he stopped her halfway. He did it very nicely with a casual: 'Oh, plenty of time to discuss that, Annis. Have you got that list of stores? Willy thinks someone ought to fetch them while the weather's good.'

She answered him in an even voice which betrayed nothing of her feelings. 'Yes, of course. But won't you have to go to the hospital before you leave?'

'No.' After a tiny pause he went on: 'Will you go to the hospital and collect some more culture tubes? We're getting low.' He nodded cheerfully at her and stumped away.

She should have enjoyed her trip to Ny Aalesund; it was a bright, chilly day and the mountains looked magnificent, even the tiny town sparkled in the sunshine. She was given a warm welcome by the shop manager and an even warmer one by the nurses when she went up to the hospital, and the pastor and his family, when she and Freddy called there for lunch, presented her with a woollen cap and mitts and a fossil, found by the children and saved specially for her. The thought that she would probably never see them again saddened her. They were so content with their lives; they had their books and radio, their beautiful handwork and the friendship of the close-knit little community. Annis thought that if only Jake were to have his home there, she would be content to stay there too.

Back at the station there was no sign of Jake. For a few panicky moments she wondered if he had already left, and then chided herself for thinking it. He wouldn't have gone without saying goodbye; he might not care twopence for her, but his manners were without fault, an opinion borne out within a short time by Harald who came in search of her while she was laying the table for breakfast.

'Jake says could you spare time to go over to the surgery? Sven's got something in his eye and he needs help.'

Annis tore off her apron and hurried across the barren ground to find Jake quietly waiting by his patient. 'Sorry about this,' he told her. 'The lamp's given out and I need a strong light—there's the big hand lamp if you'd hold it steady. It's a minute rock splinter —I've put drops in, it shouldn't take a minute.'

It took rather less. She adjusted a pad and eyeshield, entered the details neatly in the day book and started to tidy up. After Sven had gone, she thought hopefully, perhaps Jake would tell her ... Tell her what? There was no reason to tell her anything at all, and apparently he felt the same, for with brief thanks and a friendly smile, he left her to her clearing up.

Rather desperately the next day she went in search of Willy in his small office. 'I was wondering,' she began, 'when is Sven's sister coming back? I ought to make some arrangements if she's arriving soon ...'

Willy took off his spectacles the better to look at her. 'I'm not sure when, my dear,' he smiled vaguely. 'I think she'll be coming with Jake's replacement—that's —let me see, when is Jake going? Three days' time, isn't it?' He picked up his pen. 'I should ask Jake, he'll know.' He nodded happily at her, relieved not to be bothered any more, and she went away again. Everyone told her to ask Jake, but he hadn't given her the chance, had he? Perhaps there was some conspiracy to keep her there for ever.

She came across Jake the next day, down by the jetty, perched precariously on its side while two of the men serviced his plane. They all called a greeting to her, but as she wasn't invited to stay, she walked on towards the radio station, trying to look as though she had a purpose in going there. If no one had said anything by the evening, she decided, she would make Jake give her a definite date when she could leave as soon after the other girl got back as possible. She could go back by the Coastal Express, it would be an experience, and she could get a ship back to Newcastle or Harwich from Bergen. When she got back, Freddy lounged in as she was making coffee. She put a mug in his hands, well sugared, and asked firmly: 'When are you leaving, Freddy? Everyone's so vague, and that means you too.'

'Me—didn't I tell you? I'm going in Jake's plane, old girl.'

'Jake's plane?' she repeated stupidly. 'But why didn't you tell me? What about me?'

'Sven's sister's flying in with the new medical man the day after tomorrow; they'll fly you back and see you safely on your way.' He sounded a little strange, just as he used to when he was a small boy and telling fibs. She looked at him narrowly, but he returned her gaze with an innocent eye.

'You're the limit,' she told him roundly, 'going off and leaving me ... where are you going anyway?'

He got up and poured himself more coffee. 'Tromso.'

They were a devoted brother and sister, but she had never invaded his private life so she didn't ask the questions teetering on her lip. 'I expect I'll go down to Great-Aunt Mary for a few days,' she told him. She put down her mug. 'I must go and see to supper.'

No one said a word about anyone leaving over the supper table. Perhaps the men were tired; they talked in their various languages to each other and in English to her and didn't linger. She put the place to rights and then on an impulse told her two kitchen helpers that she could manage without them. There was a great pile of dishes to wash up, but in the mood she was in she really didn't care if they took her all night. But hard work didn't help; with only the knives and forks done she abandoned the sink and sat down at the kitchen table. Life had become absolutely beastly and she was fed up. She kicked the table viciously and hurt her foot, then burst into tears.

She sobbed and sniffed, her bright head on the table, and then let out a watery shriek when Jake's voice said: 'Tears? My poor little Annis!'

No one had ever called her little Annis before, the whole of her magnificent five feet ten inches was comforted by that, and he had said it with such tenderness. She mumbled something without lifting her head because her face would be blotched and puffy by now, and he asked: 'Where are you going when you leave here, Annis?'

She gave an unhappy yelp at that, looking into a future which held no Jake; it was as black and empty as a bottomless well. She lifted her head for a moment. 'Nowhere special,' she mumbled again.

'Good—I'd rather hoped for that. Annis, will you marry me?' And when she started up, her poor woebegone face open-mouthed in surprise: 'Oh, I know you're still unhappy about Ola and understand how miserable life is for you, but you will get over it, I can promise you that.' He smiled down at her. 'You're the nicest girl I have ever met and the prettiest, I like the way you walk and talk and the way you look—I enjoy being with you, I think that we could have a

happy life together. I won't rush you into anything.'
He glanced down at his plaster. 'I can't anyway with
this thing, can I?'

Annis pushed back her hair with a hand which shook
a little. 'You want to marry me?'

He said carefully: 'Yes, I do, and I'm quite prepared to wait until you've got over Ola.' He went on
slowly: 'Although I can't see any reason why we can't
marry as soon as possible—you're out of a job and now
my sister's married there's no one to look after me.'

The happiness which had been flooding her col-
lapsed like a soap bubble. He wanted someone to run
his home for him, someone he liked and already knew,
and think how useful she would be, a trained nurse . . .
The thought hurt like a knife. On the other hand, she
loved him and later she would be able to tell him that,
and if she didn't do that, she would still be able to be
with him. She longed to tell him that very instant, but
he hadn't said that he loved her; perhaps later on his
liking would turn to love and then she could explain
that she had been unhappy because she had thought
she would never see him again, not because she loved
Ola.

'You're quite sure?' she asked him.

'Quite sure.' And even though she hadn't said more
than that he pulled her gently to her feet and kissed
her gently.

'I look a fright,' said Annis.

'A little sodden, perhaps.' He mopped her face with
his handkerchief and went on matter-of-factly: 'We'll
go back by ship, we've time enough, and you can see
something of Norway.'

'You were going to fly.'

'Freddy'll take the plane back for me. Do you want to go to England first?'

She hesitated. 'Well, yes—I mean there's Great-Aunt Mary, and my clothes are at Mere.'

'Then we'll fly from Bergen and when you're ready we'll go to Goes. You can stay with my mother until we can be married.'

It was all a little breathtaking. 'How long will that be?'

'A week or so. There's not much point in hanging around.'

'No—no, of course not. Was it because your sister got married that you came here?'

His eyes looked black, sparkling with amusement. 'You could say that,' he agreed comfortably, and she nodded soberly. It was a bit off-putting to be asked to marry someone just because his sister had left him to get married and he needed someone to cook and clean, although perhaps that was a bit exaggerated; if he could afford to fly his own plane he must surely have someone to clean the house ... But she loved him and that surely made things right? She frowned a little and he said: 'Well, don't let's worry about that now; we'd better get this washing up done.'

He washed up very well while she dried and when they were half finished he observed mildly: 'Not a very romantic proposal, I'm afraid, Annis, but I don't pretend to compete with Ola—I don't intend to, either.' He bent over the sink so that she couldn't see his face. 'Do you believe in romance, my dear?'

'Not any more.' She managed to make her voice light

and when he looked at her, smiled as well. 'I'd rather be like us—good friends.' And because that didn't seem quite enough: 'And—and fond of each other.'

He didn't answer, but presently, when he said good-night to her at her hut door, his kiss, quick and hard, made her hope, foolishly enough she had to admit, that perhaps in time he might grow more than fond.

CHAPTER FIVE

FREDDY was still up. He gave Annis a quick look as she went in and put his book down. 'Been talking to Jake?' he enquired.

She hadn't meant to tell him—not yet, not until she had had time to think about it. She said now: 'I'm going back with him when he goes.'

Her brother showed no surprise. 'I thought perhaps you might; he asked me if I'd fly his plane back as he wanted to go by Coastal Express, and it crossed my mind that it might be because of you.'

'We're going to be married.'

Freddy got up and crossed the little room and kissed her cheek. 'Now that's what I call a nice piece of news! When's it to happen?'

'Well, I don't know exactly. Soon, I think.'

'Good, so it won't be dressy—it won't be a white satin and flowers affair.'

Annis, who had been contemplating just that, glared at him. 'You horrid creature, why shouldn't I wear white satin if I choose? I'm not all that old.' She looked uneasy. Jake might want a quiet wedding; after all, he was well into his thirties and probably thought of her as a sensible young woman rather than a young girl.

'You're twenty-seven,' remarked Freddy, just to clinch the matter, and then seeing his sister's dangerously glinting green eyes: 'Not that anyone would know—you're quite pretty. Jake'll make a splendid husband.'

She wanted to agree with him wholeheartedly, to tell him that Jake was the only man in the world for her, that she couldn't wait to be married to him, but something made her hold her tongue. She said mildly: 'Yes, I think he will. We're going to Mere first.'

'He'll go down a treat with Aunt Mary. Where are you getting married?'

'I've no idea.' She didn't want to talk any more, she wished Jake had been there too to answer Freddy's questions. 'I think I'll go to bed.' At the door she paused. 'Would I look silly in white satin?' she asked wistfully.

'Lord, no, not if you've set your heart on it.'

With which cold comfort she had to be content.

Jake made no secret of their engagement. She was greeted by a barrage of congratulations the next morning, but if the men hoped to see Jake display anything but his usual polite friendliness towards her, they were disappointed. His 'good morning' was exactly the same as it had always been, and in the surgery later he was so professional that she only just stopped herself in time from addressing him as Sir. It wasn't until she had made her preparations for the midday meal and had wandered across the bare ground with her coffee mug in her hand that he came swinging along on his crutches towards her. 'We leave tomorrow evening,' he told her without preamble. 'Can you be ready by then?'

She felt shy of him, which was absurd after working

with him for the last few weeks. 'Yes, easily,' and then:
'How do we go? I mean, which way will the Coastal
go?'

'It'll pick us up and go on to Longyearbyen and
then Bear Island the next day—we can't go ashore,
there's no harbour, but they send the supplies ashore,
then two days at sea before we reach Tromso. We
ought to get a chance to go ashore. We cross the Arctic
Circle the following day and probably call at several
of the smaller places before we reach Trondheim.
We'll go ashore there too and anywhere else where we
stop long enough. The next day we get to Bergen—
we'll fly to London from there. Have you sent a message
to your aunt?'

Annis looked startled. 'No—I didn't think about it.
Could I telephone when we get to Heathrow?'

'Better still, you can call her from Bergen.'

'Yes—well ... yes; she'll be surprised ...'

'Naturally. We'll have time to make our plans on
our way back. I sent a radiogram to my mother, by the
way. She is delighted and sends her warmest good
wishes.'

'How kind of her.' Annis looked into her mug as
though it might supply her with the information she
wanted. 'What is she like—your mother?'

He smiled a little. 'As tall as you and what I suppose one would call a big woman, handsome rather
than pretty, grey hair, dark eyes, excellent health. She
likes her own way. She always thought she had it while
my father was alive; he knew exactly how to treat her,
now that she is alone we do our best to keep her within

bounds, but it's sometimes difficult. Perhaps you will do better.'

Annis drew a long breath. His mother sounded pretty awful, perhaps she would take a dislike to her son's wife ... If I didn't love him so hopelessly, she thought, I'd change my mind smartly. But she did love him, enough to bear with a dozen difficult mothers. She said serenely: 'I shall do my best, Jake.' And on an afterthought: 'Your practice—have you a partner? Will you want me to help in any way?'

His firm mouth curved faintly. 'No, thanks. I've two partners and we have a secretary and a nurse and so on. I expect you'll find the house will keep you busy.'

She had a sudden vision of herself toiling round a not very modern house with a great many stairs and a semi-basement kitchen and one daily woman to do the rough. She said faintly: 'Oh, yes, I daresay I shall. Do you live in a house or an apartment?'

'Oh, a house—the town sort, you know. There's a garden and it's right in the centre, not far to the shops and so on.'

She added a picture of her struggling to make herself understood while she bought the groceries. 'I don't know a word of Dutch.'

'You'll learn quickly enough. You shall have lessons, and all my friends speak English.'

She said: 'How nice,' rather faintly and added: 'I'd better go and see to lunch and I want to check the stores before I go.'

Jake let her go without demur and she spent the next hour rather peevishly making lists for Sven's sister. Jake was a dear, but surely he could be a little more attentive? Not another Ola, of course, and his casual fondness towards her was quite a different kettle of fish from Arthur's pompous taking her for granted, but something nicely in between. She added ten tins of baked beans to her list and chided herself for being discontented. She had got what she wanted most in life, hadn't she? Jake.

She had no time to delve deeply into her feelings during the next twenty-four hours. The plane with Sven's sister and the doctor aboard arrived mid-morning and took off again almost at once with two men due for leave on board, and Annis spent the afternoon going over the stores with her successor and handing over the short list of patients requiring attention. In no time at all it was time to say goodbye to Willy and the rest of them, wave goodbye to Freddy as he zoomed away in Jake's plane, and wait for the Coastal. It arrived punctually and she had to admire the efficiency with which she, Jake and their luggage were loaded into one of the motorboats and taken out to the 'Spitzbergen Express'. There weren't many people on board, it was getting late in the summer for tourists; there were a handful of people going on leave, or visiting families in Norway, students returning to the universities and a sprinkling of tourists who were making the round trip from Bergen to Spitzbergen and back. Annis, in her small, comfortable cabin, unpacked her overnight bag and pulled a sweater over her skirt and blouse; now they were at sea it seemed a good deal colder.

Jake's cabin was close by and it wasn't until later on

that she discovered that she was the only one to have a shower to herself. Most of the cabins had to share one, but when she offered him the use of hers he only laughed, remarking that the plaster on his leg made it difficult to shower. They went along to the dining room later still, and ate with appetite. As Annis pointed out, it was a treat to eat food she hadn't cooked herself, and besides, the menu was an excellent one. They found a sheltered spot on deck afterwards and watched Spitzbergen's mountains receding behind them.

'It was fun,' said Annis suddenly. 'I loved almost all of it.'

Jake turned to look at her. 'But not quite all, my dear. You don't want to talk about it, do you?' And before she could deny that: 'Well, I won't remind you —I'm only sorry it had to happen.' He looked ferocious for a moment. 'I'll do whatever I can to make you forget.'

Annis didn't answer at once. She was trying to find the right words to tell him that she didn't need sympathy, that her affair with Ola was as cold as yesterday's potatoes, that she was more than happy to spend the rest of her life being Jake's wife. It would be crazy to tell him that she loved him. Hadn't he told her that he needed someone to replace his sister and given no indication that he felt for her any more than affection? She had her mouth open to answer him cautiously—she had even begun: 'Jake, there's something ...' when an elderly Norwegian couple rounded their corner of the deck and stopped beside them, to engage them in a friendly conversation for the next half hour, when it was then so late that all there was left to do was go below and go to bed. They had cabins close to each other too with the married couple just across the way, so that they stood together for a few minutes, saying goodnight, and since they lingered, Annis gave up all hope of Jake kissing her and with a murmured goodnight went into her cabin.

And in the morning his greeting was pleasantly friendly and nothing more. He enquired as to whether she had slept and observed that the ship would halt briefly at Bear Island and if she wanted to see all there was to see, they had better have their breakfast.

It was splendid weather still and they leaned over the ship's rail, watching the lonely place getting nearer and nearer as the ship steamed towards it. On the whole, Annis decided, she didn't mind very much not being able to land there. It looked bare and bleak and the radio station looked far lonelier than the one on Spitzbergen. Jake laughed at her and pointed out that Spitzbergen was just as bleak, only larger, although during the short summer, when the birds came briefly and the small, tough flowers bloomed, it was touched with beauty.

'Yes, I know,' agreed Annis, 'but the mountains swallow all that up, if you see what I mean. Where do we go next?'

'Tromso. We'll get there tomorrow morning—we'll go ashore if you like.'

She hesitated. 'That would be nice, but won't your leg bother you?'

'No, not a bit. We'll take a look at the Arctic Cathedral and sample the shops. If you've looked your fill of

Bear Island, let's go below and have a drink.'

The day passed pleasantly doing nothing much, making the acquaintance of the other passengers and then later in the afternoon, leaning on the rails again, warmly wrapped against the chilly wind, and it was then that Jake began to talk about their wedding.

'How do you feel about it?' he wanted to know. 'Do you hanker after a quiet ceremony—no church if you like, it's quite legal in Holland without—or shall we have a nice warm-blooded family affair with everyone invited? A good idea, actually, as then you can meet the family all at once.'

Annis remembered what Freddy had said. 'Aren't I a bit old for all that? I mean, a veil and white dress and bridesmaids?'

Jake's eyebrows shot up. 'What a ridiculous idea! You'll make a beautiful bride and I for one should like it. Would you have time to get your things ready in three weeks? I'll see to the reception and all that if you like to invite anyone you want—they can come over to Goes by plane.'

It was exciting and her eyes sparkled. It would be lovely to have a proper wedding. Then her face dropped. 'Only I haven't any family, only Great-Aunt Mary and Freddy—I've lots of friends, though.'

'Then invite them all, let me know how many there will be and I'll arrange for a plane to bring them over.'

'But that'll cost the earth—I couldn't let you . . .'

He smiled at her lazily. 'My dear girl, I only intend to marry once in my lifetime and I'd like to remember it as a special occasion—think of all the money I haven't spent while we've been at Spitzbergen. How many friends have you? Fifty? A hundred?'

'Good heavens, no!' She counted on her fingers, muttering as she did so. 'I'm not quite certain, but I can think of twenty-odd people.'

'Willy can't get away, unfortunately. A pity, but it can't be helped.'

'Ah, well. I've an uncle somewhere in Cornwall, but I haven't seen him since I was a baby and I wouldn't care to ask him.'

They wandered down for tea, still talking about the wedding, and it wasn't until they had almost finished that Annis said: 'I still don't know much about your family. Do they live near you?'

'Mother lives at Bergen-op-Zoom, about half an hour's drive away, my sister lives at s'Hertenbosch— her husband's a doctor too. I've any number of aunts and uncles and cousins—they'll all be at the wedding.' He twinkled nicely at her. 'Most of them are nice; there are one or two I don't care about, but as we seldom meet I don't suppose that'll matter. They'll be all so eager to see the bride ...'

'But, Jake,' cried Annis, 'I shall feel frightful, I don't understand a word of Dutch for a start.'

'Not to worry—everyone'll speak some sort of English.'

She said doubtfully: 'I don't know if Great-Aunt Mary would enjoy ...'

'We'll ask her. And now how about joining the Jenn-sens for that game of bridge we promised them?'

Which Annis obediently did, secretly hating it. She played badly anyway and because her mind was busy pondering the unpalatable fact that Jake, while seeming to enjoy her company, didn't seem to mind when he had to share it with anyone else, she played abominably. At the end of the second rubber, lost, like the first one, by her witless playing, she looked guiltily across the table to Jake and was put out to observe that while his face was impassive, his eyes were gleaming with wicked laughter. 'I'm not very good at bridge,' she told him with hauteur, and then had to gulp back annoyance at his:

'Never mind, my dear—what is it they say? "Unlucky at cards, lucky in love." '

He grinned at her and their companions made a few mild jokes in their almost perfect English, so that she had to smile with them while she longed to pick up the ashtray on the table and hurl it at Jake's handsome head.

Her ill temper only lasted a little while; how could she be angry with someone she loved as much as she loved Jake? She was her usual calm self for the rest of the day and on the following morning, when they arrived at Tromso, she was a perfect companion, listening to every word Jake had to say as they drove round the town and to visit the Arctic Cathedral. It was a bit off-putting when, on their return to the ship, he remarked laughingly:

'How very compliant you were, Annis. Not a single argument and you didn't contradict me once. It's a good thing I know better ...'

'What do you mean?'

'Why, that you have a mind of your own and aren't above speaking it. I don't think I should like a wife who moulded herself into my shadow.'

Annis bent to pick an invisible speck off her slacks. She would have to think about that remark presently. Now she composed her voice to nothing but pleasant amusement. 'Have no fear of that,' she assured him. 'I have no intention of being anyone's shadow—I have a headache and I suppose that made me a bit dull.'

'Oh, never dull, my dear Annis. I'm sorry about the head.' He sounded impersonally kind. 'I should go and lie down for an hour—I'll get someone to bring you a cup of tea, if you can manage to get a short nap, you should be as right as rain for the evening.'

She wanted nothing more than to be alone. She agreed eagerly, so eagerly in fact that he gave her a sharp glance from under his heavy lids. But she didn't see that, only sped to her cabin and lay down on her bunk. A cup of tea would be nice and help her to think.

An hour later she was still teasing her brain and now she had a real headache. What exactly had Jake meant when he had said that he didn't want a wife who was his shadow? Was he warning her that he wanted to lead his own life when they were married? That he didn't want her interfering in any way? No help in the surgery, no questions as to where he had been or where he was going? No requests to go with him sometimes? She couldn't guess the answers and she couldn't pluck up the courage to ask him what he meant. He had told her that he wanted to marry her and because she loved him she had said she would, half believing that he loved her—not very much perhaps, but still enough to make their marriage successful. Now she wasn't sure.

She got up and changed into a plain jersey dress and picked up the woollen stole he had bought her that morning. It was chilly in the evenings once the sun started to go down and she was grateful for it, and she was thankful too that its delicate pink gave her face some colour. Staring at her reflection, she decided that she looked a hag; all eyes and pallor.

But judging from the look Jake gave her when she joined him presently, she couldn't have looked as bad as all that. The sight of him sent her headache flying, and the evening, which she had been dubious about, became a delight.

They went to the island of Hinnoya the next day and landed briefly at Harstad before going on to Sortland and Stokmarknes and then through the Raftsundet channel to cross the Arctic Circle, and then, with Trondheim only a day away, to go ashore at Sandnessjoen.

At Trondheim they spent several hours sightseeing; the cathedral, a massive sombre building of magnificence, the royal palace, the quaint old houses in the town and of course the shops. They bought things here—painted wooden bowls and trays, hand-knitted woollies for Great-Aunt Mary, a pair of gloves Annis liked and several pieces of glass she admired. Jake was in high spirits and Annis, packing everything tidily away in her luggage later, longed for him to be like that always. He wouldn't be, of course, but it had been wonderful and she had loved every minute of his lighthearted banter and gentle teasing.

They took a look at Kristiansund on the following day too and bought some pottery figures, although as Annis protested, there wasn't an inch of space left in their luggage, and then finally they were at Bergen.

It was after lunch when they arrived and they went straight to an hotel. 'We'll spend the night here,' Jake had told her, 'so you can have a quick look round and catch a morning plane to Heathrow. While you're settling in I'll see about it.'

He bought her a silver bracelet later, while they were strolling round the shops before dinner that evening. It was a beautiful thing and if she hadn't been firm, he would have bought her anything else she had fancied. They had a drink in a pleasant little bar near the water and then strolled back to the hotel with Jake handling his crutches so inconspicuously that she forgot now and then that he was using them. He didn't seem to tire at all, either, and if she asked him, he brushed her concern aside with a faint impatience, so that after a while she had learned not to say anything. But that evening as they sat over dinner he remarked casually that he would be glad when he got back to Goes and could get a walking iron fixed. 'I can manage with a stick then,' he pointed out. 'I'll have to use it at our wedding, I'm afraid—I hope you won't mind?'

'Not a bit. How long will it be before you can discard the walking plaster?'

He shrugged. 'It rather depends—not many weeks, I should imagine; I'll know more when I've had another X-ray.'

With that she had to be content. She knew that he intended working the moment he returned and she didn't think that he would allow a mere leg in plaster to make much difference to his life; perhaps there would be someone to drive him round to his patients. For the first time she found herself wondering if he had had a lot of girl-friends and whether they would mind him marrying her. She would have liked to have asked him but something stopped her; he had been tact itself over Ola, and although he had dismissed Arthur as of no importance, he had never asked a lot of tiresome questions; so she mustn't either.

It was funny to be back in England the next day. Heathrow was choked with people, but Jake made his way unhurriedly through the crowds, conjured up a porter, took Annis through Customs and then into the enormous reception hall. They hadn't crossed more than ten feet of it before a middle-aged man in a neat blue suit joined them.

Jake leaned on his crutches and put a hand on Annis's arm. 'Here's Cor—he'll take care of everything.' And he spoke to the man in his own language.

Annis stood watching them; she had no idea who Cor might be, but she supposed that she would be told in time. He seemed quiet and sensible, listening to what Jake had to say without interruption before he turned to her as Jake said: 'Annis, this is Cor, my friend and chauffeur and steward. He's also my right hand, he'll be yours too.'

Annis held out a hand and Cor shook it gently and said in stilted English: 'I am so glad to meet Miss Brown and offer my best wishes for her happiness.' He added, still in English to Jake: 'You wish to go to the car, Doctor?'

Jake nodded and they started off again, making for the entrance and the road outside. There were a great many cars lining the road. Annis glanced around her and wondered which one was Jake's; the big white Merc, perhaps, or the dark blue BMW parked behind it. It was neither of these, it was the dark grey Bristol 303, its dignified lines and unobtrusive class making the other two cars appear showy. I might have known, thought Annis, and obediently started to get in beside the driver's seat. Half way there she paused. 'Yes, but what about you, Jake?'

He waved to a pile of letters which were stacked on the back seat. 'You won't mind? I can get these read and some of them dealt with while we travel. I've told Cor to stop when he sees an empty phone box for you. It would be hopeless to try from here. He knows the way, I asked him to make sure of that, though I expect he'll want your help when we get to Mere.'

He smiled at her, a warm friendly smile which seemed to take it for granted that she found everything just as satisfactory as he did, and got into the back of the car. Minutes later they were on their way.

And minutes later they stopped so that Annis might do her telephoning, armed with the handful of tenpenny pieces Jake had thoughtfully offered her. Great-Aunt Mary was home and being herself, remained unflurried when Annis told her news, beyond saying that she was delighted and would trout, jacket potatoes and a bottle of that Hock she had been saving for some special occasion do for their suppers. Annis said that it sounded lovely and mentioned Cor.

'I'll get a room for him at the Wool and Whistle,'

said Great-Aunt Mary. 'Can this young man of yours get himself upstairs with that plaster on his leg or shall I give him a shakedown in the drawing room?'

Annis dismissed a picture of Jake trying to fit his size into the little room. 'He can manage stairs very well,' she said firmly, 'in fact you don't remember about his leg most of the time.' She put another coin in. 'I'd better go now, they're waiting for me just outside and it's quite a busy road.'

Her aunt made an agreeing sound and then asked: 'Freddy? Is he with you? I had a postcard about three weeks ago—he said he'd be leaving soon.'

'He's not here, he's flying back—I'll tell you later. He's fine.' Annis added 'bye' quickly before her aunt could think of anything else to say and went back to the car.

Neither of its occupants appeared impatient; she was smilingly reinstated beside Cor, asked by Jake if she wanted to stop anywhere on their way, and when she said no, she didn't think so, was gently told to sit back and enjoy the ride.

Which she did. Cor was surprisingly well-informed about everything, she could only suppose Jake took him into his confidence about most things. He had, he said, never been to Spitzbergen although he hoped to do so one day. Norway he knew fairly well; he had been there during the war, fighting with the Norwegians because he had been staying with an aunt who lived at Narvik. 'And naturally, miss, I got to know the country, moving around as we did.'

He was nice, Annis decided, and his manner was exactly right. She had never had anything much to do with servants, but she was forcefully reminded of an old-fashioned family retainer who, while never overstepping his place, was all part and parcel of that same family. One day, when she had got to know him better, she would ask him how long he had been with Jake.

They were on the point of leaving the M3 when Jake spoke quietly from the back. 'Cor, make for Middle Wallop, will you? I'm sure Annis would like tea and I've a fancy to see a place with a name like that.' He added: 'Fifehead Manor, Cor.'

Cor answered him in Dutch and they both laughed gently as Cor sent the car surging ahead.

Fifehead Manor was a country house, and the tea it served was elegant; the three of them sat devouring cucumber sandwiches, fruit cake and tiny sugar-topped cakes while Annis wielded the teapot. As she put her cup down she said wonderingly: 'Cor, you're awfully good at finding your way—have you been here before?'

His nice face wrinkled into a smile. 'No, Miss Brown; the doctor told me exactly where we should be going and all I had to do was look at my map.'

'Oh, I see.' She looked at Jake. 'Do you usually drive yourself? I mean, when your legs are O.K.?'

He smiled slowly. 'Always, my dear. Shall we go? If you're ready?'

As she directed Cor off the road at Mere and told him to park a few yards down the narrow lane, she wondered what Jake would think of Great-Aunt Mary's house, but she had no time to worry about that as she led the way down the little path by the stream with cottages on the further side of it, each with its own little plank bridge. Riverside Cottage looked small but very pretty as they reached it, and: 'Mind the planks,' warned Annis as she went across and then turned back. 'Jake, can you manage? If I take a crutch and you hold the rail?'

But he managed very well without anyone's help and they went through the wooden gate and up the short path to the porch. There was no need to knock, Great-Aunt Mary had flung open the door and was waiting for them.

She embraced Annis first, said in a clarion voice: 'No ring, Annis?' and then turned to Jake. 'Jake? I am delighted to meet you—what a very large man you are, to be sure. Come inside—and this is Cor?' She shook hands and retired into the narrow little hall so that they could get in too, then ushered them into her tiny drawing room, charming with its flower-patterned curtains and Victorian furniture. It seemed even tinier with Jake in it, looking dubiously at the crinoline chairs which would most certainly collapse under his weight. His hostess interpreted his glance and observed in her brisk way: 'You'd better sit on the sofa, Jake, it's a stout piece belonging to my grandfather,' she added: 'Annis, you didn't mention what a very large man he is.'

Annis had perched on one of the velvet-covered chairs. 'No—well, I didn't think ... that is, I'm used to Jake being big and I hardly notice ...'

He came to her rescue. 'I hope you won't notice either, Miss Brown, or at least, I hope you will get used to me once I'm in the family.'

Great-Aunt Mary looked him over and then smiled at him. 'I think I shall like you and I daresay you're just what Annis needs. We'll have a drink to that.'

The drink was home-made parsnip wine and Annis, sipping cautiously because she knew how potent it was, watched Jake's face as he tasted it. To his credit his expression didn't change, although his eyes darkened with amusement, and as for Cor, he prudently waited until everyone else had tasted it before trying it himself.

'Delicious,' pronounced Jake. 'You make all your own wines, Miss Brown?'

'Call me Great-Aunt Mary,' said that lady gruffly. 'Yes, I do—you shall take a bottle back with you.'

Which they did, after two days of planning and telephoning and finding someone to look after Tim the cat while Miss Brown would be at the wedding. Cor disappeared discreetly each day, appearing miraculously whenever he was needed and Jake—Jake, Annis had to admit, was a great success with her aunt, just as he was a great success with her. He might not be a very romantic man, but he made her feel wanted ...

They had decided to spend a day in London on the way back so that Annis could buy her wedding dress and meet Carol, who had agreed excitedly to be a bridesmaid, and it was still fairly early in the morning when they left Mere and Cor set the Bristol racing towards London. And this time Annis sat in the back with Jake, making lists and doing sums, while he listened idly to her mutterings. She didn't suppose he was very interested in what she intended to wear, but he was too polite to say so. He argued the superiority of organza over crêpe-de-chine, agreed that a short veil was much prettier than a long one and asked her what flowers she wished to carry. The journey passed very pleasantly and after lunch at Claridges she was put in Cor's care and driven to Carol's little flat in Highgate, where the two girls spent a feverish hour discussing the wedding.

They went shopping the next day and Annis, quite carried away with an excitement she tried to suppress, bought a creamy organza gown and the short veil Jake preferred. It took most of the morning and she would have happily gone on buying, only Jake reminded her gently that they were crossing to Holland that evening and anything else she wanted she could buy just as easily there. 'We'll go shopping together,' he promised her, and smiled his slow, friendly smile.

She had really had no time to enjoy the hotel or its luxuries, she thought, getting ready for bed on the ferry later. Everything had been done in such a rush, and yet Jake hadn't appeared to hurry her at all, perhaps it was because so much had happened in so short a time. She curled up in her bunk going over the conversations they had had; he had been sweet and charmingly thoughtful of her, but now she had time to ponder everything, he hadn't kissed her once; not since they had arrived in England. She frowned and slept.

CHAPTER SIX

THEY arrived so early in the morning at Vlissingen that there was no time and no inclination for breakfast. Annis had a cup of tea in her cabin and then joined Jake and Cor as the disembodied voice from the loudspeakers asked everyone to go to their cars. There was no delay; they were off the ferry, through Customs and driving down a narrow unpaved lane before she had quite realised that they were actually in Holland.

'About half an hour,' said Jake beside her, 'it's motorway all the way.' He smiled. 'It's a pleasant morning in which to see Holland for the first time.'

And indeed it was; the pearly sky was pinkened by the sun's rays and the flat green land lay serene around them. Annis could see factory chimneys in the distance and the fringe of Middelburg, its orderly rows of suburban houses and apartments concealing the lovely heart of the city.

Jake sat back in his corner, watching her, telling her a little of the country they were passing through until he observed: 'There's the T.V. tower at Goes,' and said something to Cor in his own language. Cor laughed as he answered him and Annis suddenly felt scared; Jake's mother, until that moment a nebulous figure in the safely distant future, was here, waiting for her. Panic churned her insides and she let out a held breath when he said placidly: 'Feeling scared,

Annis? No need.' He put out a hand and took hers in it, engulfing it comfortingly. 'The town centre is down that street we're just passing, we go down the next one.'

It was a wide thoroughfare, tree-lined and with rather heavy red brick houses set in well-cared-for gardens, and she was conscious of a vague disappointment. She had expected something really Dutch, like a picture of one of the Old Masters. She wasn't disappointed. Cor sent the car down a narrow road which took them back towards the town's centre and presently it opened into a narrow street beside a wide canal lined with trees, and beyond them, facing the water, houses, tall and narrow with gabled roofs topping their three or four storeys. Cor stopped the car before one of the tallest, its great windows surrounded by elaborate plaster work, its massive door heavily carved.

'Home,' said Jake, and bent and kissed her gently before giving her back her hand.

Cor went ahead of them, across the brick pavement, then opened the door and stood aside for them to go inside. A glass vestibule opened into a narrow lofty hall, carpeted in a rich shade of burgundy, its white-painted walls lighted by crystal sconces, and at one side, under a wide arch, Annis caught a glimpse of a staircase. Walking beside Jake as he stomped along on his gutter crutches, she thought how different it was from what she had imagined it might be—and then didn't think at all as he leaned forward and opened a door at the end of the hall.

The room was square and not too large, its high ceiling adorned with strap work, its walls panelled in some dark wood. There was a distinctly Victorian flavour about its furniture; a round rosewood table stood in the centre of the fine carpet, there were glass-fronted bookcases on either side of the marble fire-place, and the chairs arranged here and there were large, comfortable and covered in rich velvets.

A lady was seated in one of these chairs, very up-right. She was grey-haired and elderly and, Annis saw with a sinking heart, of majestic appearance. And when she rose to her feet it was apparent that she was as tall as Annis, rather stout and possessed of handsome rather than good looks, just as her son had said. Annis, taking in the expensive, beautifully cut dress, thought rather defiantly that she wouldn't allow herself to be intimidated by Jake's formidable mother—far worse than she had imagined. Jake's cheerful voice broke up her thoughts: 'Mama, how nice of you to be waiting for us—so early too.' He bent to kiss her cheek. 'And here is Annis.'

How bald, thought Annis; here's Annis, take her or leave her. She held out a hand and smiled nicely be-cause after all she did love Jake very much, enough to put up with a rather fierce-looking mother-in-law if she had to.

But it wasn't like that at all. Jake's mother took her hand and then bent her head to kiss her warmly. 'My dear child,' she declared in vibrant tones, 'you have no idea how delighted I am—the whole family too, that Jake has found himself a wife, and such a pretty one too.' She beamed down at her. 'And doubly welcome because you are English. My husband's mother was an Englishwoman and indeed, there have been any number married into the family over the years. Now do let us have breakfast and then Jake can go away and do whatever he wants and we can have a nice little talk.'

Annis murmured something and Jake agreed placidly; he would always agree placidly, decided Annis, unless it was something he didn't want to do, and then nothing would make him do it. She allowed herself to be led back into the hall by a strapping pink-cheeked girl in a cotton dress and a very clean white apron, whose name was Ellie, and through the arch and up the oak staircase curving to the next floor where she was shown into a room overlooking the garden at the back of the house. It was at the end of a long narrow passage, with other passages leading from it, some with a step or two up or down, so that she was a little doubtful of finding her way down again but she didn't worry about that; the room was worth a little journey; it wasn't too large and it was very light by reason of the enormous window draped in pale chintz, it was furnished with a little canopied bed, a walnut sofa table with a triple gilded mirror upon it, a tallboy, also of walnut, and a comfortable chair or two The two doors in its damask-hung walls led to a very large clothes closet and a bathroom which lacked, as far as she could see, nothing at all. She explored slowly and then, in a panic that she would keep the others waiting, did her face and hair and started off on the return journey. She had reached the end of the passage when she heard Jake's mild bellow: 'Annis? Turn left when you reach the small landing and go through the archway—the staircase is there.'

And so it was, or at least a branch of it, the rest wandered off in quite another direction. She reached the bottom and found him waiting for her.

'You shall have a conducted tour later,' he promised her. 'The house is a rabbit warren, but we don't notice it, having lived in it all our lives. I'm going down to the hospital presently and then on to see my partners; you'll be all right with my mother?'

She said oh yes, of course, and hoped she sounded as certain of it as he obviously expected her to be, not sure whether to be relieved or hurt at his careless friendliness. The memory of Ola caught her in a little gust of regret; she had no feeling for him any more, but she couldn't forget the romance of it all. And just as though he had read her thoughts, Jake said softly: 'You'll forget, my poor dear, I swear you will—I'll see to that.'

She looked up at him, on the verge of telling him that there wasn't anything to forget; she even began: 'Jake ...' but he interrupted her with: 'You'll feel more the thing when you've had breakfast.'

Which she did. There was nothing like a cup of excellent coffee to pull one together; she found herself enjoying rolls and butter and toast and answering Mevrouw van Germert's measured questions readily enough. The feeling that she was going to like that lady was growing stronger every minute; she might look formidable, but she was surprisingly kind and the kindness was genuine, with no attempt to ingratiate herself, and although some of her questions were searching they were born of natural curiosity and nothing else. Presently Jake left them, with a swift kiss on the cheek for Annis and the same salute for his parent. He would be back in an hour or so, he told them, and perhaps they could get some plans made while he was away.

'And you can ignore that,' said his mother as he went out of the room. 'Jake will have made all the plans he thinks necessary and will merely listen patiently to what we have to say and then go his own way. He always has.'

Annis said nothing. Somehow or other, however long it took, she would make Jake fall in love with her; not just the friendly affection he felt for her now, but a good blazing fire of feeling, and until then she was prepared to ignore everything else. She listened serenely to her companion explaining the procedure of marriage in Holland, not taking in much of it, volunteered the information that Jake had suggested a family wedding and that she had agreed, and allowed Mevrouw van Germert to embark on a list of van Germert relations who would expect to be invited. It was a long list; it took her until Ellie came in with the morning coffee.

Jake wasn't back by lunch time. They ate it in the dining room, a large room with an oval table, seating a dozen persons, a carved side-table and a William and Mary display cabinet of great beauty between the windows.

'You will be wondering,' observed Mevrouw van Germert, as she passed a critical eye over the dish of aubergine au gratin she was being offered, 'why I am here, because this is not my home, as you possibly know. It is at Jake's express wish.' She threw Annis a quick glance. 'You probably also know that he is a man of strong views. He has asked that I stay here until your marriage, but I have suggested, and I hope you will agree to this, that you might like to spend a week with me in a few days' time. Jake will be busy and have very little time to take you round and you might be lonely. You think it a good idea?'

Annis didn't think it was, but she had no intention of saying so. She would have liked nothing better than to have stayed with Jake in his house, getting to know him and his home and the people in it, but that wouldn't do.

'I should like that,' she told her hostess, 'and it's kind of you to ask me. I could have stayed at home, but Jake thought it would be a good idea if I were to find my feet before we got married.'

'Such a sensible boy,' declared his fond parent. 'His sister has been living here and looking after him, but she is married now and although he has a good house-keeper, she is quite elderly—she was a young woman when I came here as a bride, and to get another younger woman while Katrina is still alive would be cruel.'

'And so he's marrying me instead ...' Annis spoke silently, but she didn't feel sorry for herself; it was a challenge. She agreed pleasantly and remarked upon the strong resemblance between Jake and the severe, beetle-browed gentleman whose portrait was hanging on the wall opposite her.

'His great grandfather—a doctor, of course. He had a nasty temper, so I am told. Jake has a nasty temper too. Sooner or later you will get a taste of it, my dear.'

Mevrouw van Germert nodded a regal head. 'I quickly learned to ignore his dear father's little outbursts—I'm sure you will do the same with Jake.' She smiled gently. 'We will have our coffee in the drawing room and then I will show you the paintings there—they're rather fine.'

The afternoon passed pleasantly. Annis studied portrait after portrait of Jake's forebears and saw him in all of them; really, not a single one of them had missed out on the craggy features and the dark brows. She studied the charming flower paintings too and several winter scenes. She supposed that they were valuable but didn't like to ask; she had a feeling that Mevrouw van Germert had a mind above money. It was a little frightening to find that Jake was so rich. Her own people had lived comfortably enough, but certainly not on his scale, and she hoped that she would be able to live up to it; certainly she would enjoy spending money, buying beautiful clothes and taking a taxi instead of a bus; she might even have a car of her own. She wasn't a mercenary girl, but the idea was distinctly pleasant.

After tea she went up to her room, to find that someone had unpacked for her, so that all she had to do was to take a bath and change her dress. Mervouw van Germert had told her that there would only be the three of them and that a short dress would do, which was a mercy, since Annis had brought only a long evening skirt with her and a couple of silk blouses to go with it. She would have to go out in the morning and buy something ... She got into the silvery grey silk jersey which offset her hair and eyes so well, put on the strapped sandals with their ridiculous high heels and went downstairs, not hurrying in case she tripped up in them. She was on the last graceful curve of the staircase when she saw Jake watching her from the hall. He was sitting in a high-backed chair, his crutches on the floor beside him. Before she could reach him he had picked them up and was standing to meet her.

'Hullo, my dear. You look good enough to eat. Have you enjoyed your day?'

'Very much.' She was surprised to find that she had. 'And you?'

He bent and kissed her before he replied. 'Oh, yes, I enjoyed my day too. I've had my leg looked at and we've decided to keep the walking iron for another month; the tib's fine but the fib's not quite as it should be,' and at her anxious look: 'No, nothing wrong, just being slow to knit.' He began to walk along the hall beside her. 'I've settled all the forms and so on for our wedding—three weeks tomorrow. Mama will see to the actual reception and so on, I'll see about the church ceremony—all you will have to do is let us have a list of people you would like to come. Would you like to go over to England before we're married? Clothes? Go into a huddle with the bridesmaid? Hairdresser ... what else do girls do when they get married?'

She laughed. 'All those, but I don't think I need to go back. I'll buy what I want here and I shall only need my hair trimmed, I do it myself.'

He stopped to look at her. 'Your hair is glorious. Do you mean to say it curls like that without any of the hairdresser's arts?'

'Well, yes.' She couldn't think of anything else to say; he had paid her two compliments in as many minutes and he had sounded exactly like Freddy when he, on rare occasions, told her she looked all right. Probably Jake looked at her with the same brotherly eye as Freddy, she brooded gloomily, and wished heartily that she had had a new dress to put on—something to make him raise those thick eyebrows of his.

But it was impossible to feel gloomy for more than a few minutes. Dinner was a lively meal with Mevrouw van Germert full of ideas and plans while Jake sat back, smiling and listening, and Annis, quite carried away by the idea of a big wedding, joined in enthusiastically. Over coffee in the drawing room later she produced her list of guests, a small one compared to her hostess's, who explained that the family was a large one and if one invited one cousin or uncle one must invite all the others. 'You will be at my house, of course,' she decreed, 'and Jake will fetch you ...'

'Oh, will he?' asked Annis faintly. 'But what about being given away and all that?'

Jake laughed. 'We do it rather differently in Holland, my dear. The groom goes to the bride's house with her flowers and they go to the Raadhuis together, everyone else goes first.' He grinned at her. 'Will you mind stomping up the aisle with me on crutches?'

'Heavens, no.' She smiled back at him, rather mistily; it could have been so much worse than a fractured leg—head injuries, a broken back ...

'For a bride,' said Jake very softly, 'you're looking uncommonly sad.'

She shook her head. 'I'm not. Are you going back

to work straight away?'

'Tomorrow morning. I'm afraid we shan't see much of each other, but I'll take you down to the consulting rooms one morning, and the hospital—not a large one, but very efficient. I sometimes go to Utrecht and Amsterdam and the Hague, too, you must come along.'

'I'd like that.' She glowed at the thought that he wanted her company.

'Mama will be here until the end of the week,' went on Jake. 'When she goes back I thought it would be nice if you stayed with her. I'll see you each day, of course.'

She agreed pleasantly; he had arranged it all already and she wanted to do exactly what he wished. She wasn't going to be a doormat with no mind of her own, but on the other hand, she wasn't going to go against him without good reason. Presently she went up to bed; her future mother-in-law had given her a warm kiss as they said goodnight, much warmer than Jake's.

The week went quickly—there was so much to do; the house to explore, sometimes with Mevrouw van Germert, sometimes with Cor or the housekeeper, and just once or twice, with Jake. It was beautiful and it was loved as well, its many rooms still furnished with pieces which had been made when the house had been built, polished and smooth with their age. What was more, they were used. Annis, smoothing a careful hand down old damask curtains and touching the silver on the massive side-table, knew that she was going to love the house just as much as Jake so obviously did.

She went with him to his surgery too, in the heart of

the little town. It took up the whole of the ground
floor of an old house let out as offices. His partners
welcomed her with patent pleasure—Wim, the younger
of the two, and Huib, married and only a little younger
than Jake. It was a busy practice with many patients
living in the small villages around Goes, and as Jake
was at pains to explain, it was the other two who did
most of the work, because he was engaged on research
work which took up a good deal of his time. Annis met
the receptionist too, a young woman who had been
with them for some time, and the nurse, a middle-
aged housewife who ran her home and the practice
with equal efficiency. And watching Jake talking to
them, immaculate in his dark suit and sober tie, it was
hard to equate him with the sweater-clad man on
Spitzbergen, although he himself hadn't changed. She
wondered now how she could ever have disliked him,
even briefly. And even more she wondered how she
could ever have thought that she was in love with Ola.
Life, thought Annis, nipping down the narrow passage
ahead of Jake so that he had room to use his crutches,
was very strange. And exciting; there was always the
challenge of making him love her. She turned as they
reached the waiting Cor and the car to smile at him
and say: 'It's all so different, isn't it? Don't you miss
Spitzbergen?'

'Yes; life was simple there, wasn't it? One day we'll
go back there, but not yet.' His dark eyes had rested
on her face and she knew that he was remembering
Ola.

By the end of the week she was beginning to feel at
home. She knew the several servants by name, could

find her way round the old house without getting lost and had made friends with Mike, the Irish wolfhound, as well as the kitchen cats. She had gone shopping too, refusing Jake's offer to drive her to the Hague or Amsterdam, for as she pointed out sensibly, she didn't want a great deal; undies and one or two dresses and slacks and sweaters. They wouldn't be going on a honeymoon; it would have meant taking Cor with them to drive the car, since she still had to apply for a driving licence. They would travel later, Jake had promised her, and she had been content with that. Just being with him would do very nicely; she didn't ask for more.

The move to Mevrouw van Germert's house was made majestically in a large BMW because, as she observed to Annis, she liked to travel comfortably. A short square man was at the wheel and was introduced as Hans. He loaded Mevrouw van Germert's luggage into the trunk, helped her in with care, did the same for Annis and got behind the wheel where he sat patiently while Cor had a few last words with Annis and Mevrouw van Germert. Jake wasn't there; he had left the house early, although he had left a message to say that he would see them both that evening.

The BMW proceeded at a stately pace through the centre of the town and out the other side and, rather to Annis's surprise, picked up speed on the main road, leaving the town behind them.

'Have we far to go?'

'No, my dear, it's not too far away. Just this side of Bergen-op-Zoom. We have a small house in the Wouwse Plantage which is this side of the town. My husband left it to me during my lifetime; it has always been the custom for the wife, if she is widowed, to leave the house in Goes to the eldest son, so that his wife may live there with him without the hampering presence of a mother-in-law. I find it a splendid idea.'

It was, but Annis wasn't sure if it would be quite polite to agree. She said with some diplomacy: 'I hope we shall see you often, Mevrouw van Germert.'

'I shall come when you invite me, my dear,' said her companion crisply, and went on: 'This is a dull road, but the country is very pretty presently.'

She was right. Once across the narrow neck of land between Goes and Bergen there were small woods, even a hill or two, and pretty little villas tucked in between them. A few miles short of Bergen Hans took a side road towards the Belgian border and after five minutes' drive turned into a sandy lane between trees. The house at the end of it was much smaller than the one in Goes and quite different, with an elaborate roof all gables and little windows and balconies, and a pretty garden.

'Very quiet,' stated Mevrouw van Germert, 'and safe from traffic; excellent for the children.' She smiled and her handsome face softened. 'Jake must have climbed every tree here, I daresay his sons will do the same.'

Annis blushed, not because she was shy about future children but because she felt guilty because Jake's mother didn't know that he was marrying her more for convenience than anything else. She got out of the car, resolving that she and Jake would have to have a talk. The prospect of a little Jake and perhaps a sister to even things up didn't worry her in the least, indeed, she liked the idea very much, but Jake might have different ideas.

The house inside was pretty, its furniture mostly Regency, its delicate lines surprisingly at variance with Mevrouw van Germert's imposing person. They went at once to a small sitting room, where they perched on unlikely gilt chairs while an elderly woman served them sherry. 'Antonia,' introduced Mevrouw van Germert. 'She has been with me a long time now.' She sipped for a few moments. 'You shall go to your room presently, my dear. Look upon this house as your temporary home, I hope you will be happy here.'

She had spoken so kindly that Annis got up and went to kiss her cheek with an involuntary: 'How kind you are! You know so little about me and yet you have made me welcome.'

Mevrouw van Germert patted the sofa beside her and Annis sat down.

'But you are welcome. Oh, my dear, if you knew the number of times I have had to welcome Jake's girlfriends and how I longed to show them the door. Beautiful creatures, all of them, and not one of them loving Jake. Just, I am happy to say, as he didn't love any of them. All the same, I had some bad moments.'

Annis took a gulp of sherry and told herself she was a fool to mind about Jake's girl-friends. He was good-looking enough and rich enough to pick and choose —besides, his mother had said that he hadn't loved one of them. She went upstairs presently to the charming room prepared for her and sat down on the bed. She gave herself a lecture on being jealous about something she knew almost nothing about—after all, it could have been Mevrouw van Germert's own opinion of the girls—and promised herself that she wouldn't think any more about it. She didn't keep it, of course. The rest of the day was filled with speculation, doubt and a vague unhappiness, despite the fact that most of it was filled with an inspection of the house and the garden, and a long session with her hostess, looking through a family album in which photos of Jake in various stages of growing up predominated.

He came that evening, after dinner, and she felt shy of him as well as peevish. He was quick to see it and she realised that for each time she looked at him he was staring at her with half amused speculation. When his mother went away presently to telephone, he wasted no time.

'You look ready to burst into tears, Annis. What's happened? Aren't you happy to come here?'

'I'm very happy here,' she told him stiffly, and bent her head to murmur to Mike, who had come with him.

'Then it's something I've done—or not done?' he persisted. 'Come on, don't be a silly girl—tell!'

Just like Freddy, she thought bitterly. Why did men always call one a silly girl when all one wanted was a little sympathy?

'There's nothing to tell.'

'No?' He got up and came across the room to her and pulled her to her feet, wrapped his arms around her, gutter crutches and all, and kissed her gently. 'Well?'

It was impossible to keep silent. 'You've had so many girl-friends,' she muttered miserably into his shoulder.

'So why pick on me ...?'

His eyes were dark and she couldn't read the expression in them. 'Isn't it obvious, my dear Annis? I didn't want to marry any of them, but I do want to marry you.' His hands tightened on her. 'None of them were serious.'

Which made her feel mean because he could so easily have reminded her of Ola and he hadn't. She managed to smile. 'I'm sorry, I am a fool, aren't I—It's just that I'm not quite used to it all, I expect.'

He took his arms away and put one hand into a pocket. 'Which reminds me, this may make you feel it's all deadly serious.' He took out a little box and opened it. There was a ring inside, a huge sapphire surrounded by diamonds. 'I hope it fits, it's old and been in the family for years.' He slipped it on her finger. 'Good, it does. We must go shopping for wedding rings, mustn't we?'

Annis had done some shopping while she had been in Goes, one or two pretty dresses, a jersey top and skirt, some super slacks and several silk blouses. The boutique had been expensive, but she felt justified in being extravagant; one didn't marry all that often. And she bought boots too, long tan ones which showed off her long legs to perfection, as well as a pair of high-heeled pumps. She was glad she had now, for when Jake came the following evening he suggested that they might go out. 'Put on a pretty dress,' he told her. 'I'm going to take you to Schudderbeurs—it's a small hotel on the other side of Zierikzee and run by a charming couple.'

The Bristol made short work of the journey through

the early September dusk; the lights of the hotel twinkled invitingly as they drew up before its open door. Inside it was charming, pleasantly warm, dimly lighted and with a wood fire smouldering in its great open hearth. Originally an inn, it had been modernised so well that it was impossible to see the difference. Mevrouw Bouteka met them as they went in, shook their hands, assured them that she had a table ready for them and invited them to sit by the hearth and have a drink while they chose something to eat. The chairs were comfortable and the Madeira excellent. Annis felt happiness steal over her, listening to Jake telling some trifling story about one of his partner's children. They ate presently—lobster Thermidor, with avocado pear stuffed with shrimps first and fresh fruit salad with lashings of cream to follow it.

'What a heavenly place,' said Annis, pouring their coffee. 'Do you come here often?'

He smiled at her and said deliberately: 'I've brought various girl-friends here from time to time. It's cosy, isn't it?'

Her little glow of happiness flickered and died. She supposed he had brought her here because all the other girls had liked it. She said shortly: 'Very cosy. Will you have some more coffee?'

He passed his cup. 'Thanks. You look nice in that dress—did you buy it in Goes?'

'Yes, a very nice boutique down a side street, I forget its name.'

'We'll go up to den Haag when we're married and you can buy anything you want.' He put down his cup. 'I quite forgot to ask you. Have you any money?'

'Yes, thank you, quite enough.'

He stared at her, his eyes narrowed. 'Now I wonder what I've done ...'

Annis opened her green eyes very wide. 'Done? Nothing at all.' She looked around her. 'This is a delightful place.'

'You said that just now,' he reminded her, and leaned back in his chair, very much at his ease. 'Since you like it so much, we must come here often. By the way, I forgot to tell you there will be two English girls at the wedding, they're married to two friends of mine—one lives in Zierikzee and the other in Middelburg. I think you'll like them.'

'Oh, how nice! Have they been here long?'

'A few years now.' He looked across to where Mevrouw Bouteka was sitting at a small table in the middle of the restaurant, writing, and she got up and came over to them and gave him the bill. 'Don't go before Arie has seen you,' she begged. 'He'll be out in a minute.'

So they stayed another half an hour, talking to the proprietor before they finally took their leave. They drove home in almost complete silence and when they reached the house they went in together, still not speaking.

In the hall Jake said: 'I don't think I'll stay, my dear. I'm off to Utrecht in the morning just for a couple of days and I must make an early start.'

Annis hadn't expected that. All the way back she had been telling herself crossly that she didn't care if she didn't see him for days; let him take out one of those girl-friends of his—and now that he was going away even for so short a time, she was miserable. She longed to ask him why he was going, but since he never volunteered any information unless she did ask, she hesitated. She said lamely: 'Oh, are you?' And then in a rush: 'We're getting married in twelve days' time ...'

He stood in front of her, leaning on his crutches. 'I hadn't forgotten, my dear.' He bent and kissed her with sudden urgency so that she kissed him back before she could stop herself. She said goodnight then, and started for the stairs, not looking back, so that she didn't see the smile on his face.

It was three days before she saw him again and this time his kiss was a casual light affair on one cheek. All the same, she was so happy to see him again that she didn't care; just seeing him was enough. He told her a little of what he'd been doing, too. 'Though there's still a lot to do,' he observed. 'Research is something which lasts one's lifetime.'

'You like it better than G.P.'s work?'

He considered. 'It's absorbing, but then so are the patients. I suppose I like them equally. I heard from Willy yesterday, he's coming to see us in a few weeks' time; he said the station isn't the same without you.'

She laughed. 'I can't believe that. It was fun, though. Freddy wants to go back.'

'There's always a place for a good man. Do you want to go out or shall we stay here and dine with Mama?'

She chose to stay. His face was lined with tiredness; he could relax in his mother's house, he could even go to sleep if he wanted to while Annis and Mevrouw van Germert gossiped. They had become good friends during the past days. Annis, who had heard dreadful things about mothers-in-law, had been delighted about that.

They didn't go out on any of the ensuing nights, either, there were suddenly a lot of last-minute arrangements to make, packing to do, her hair to be seen to, telephone calls and endless priming from Mevrouw van Germert as to her future relations. And on the evening before the wedding everyone arrived and in the rush of meeting them, seeing them safely into their hotels and installing Great-Aunt Mary and Carol in two of the guest rooms, she hardly had time to speak to Jake who arrived in time for dinner, but only just. It was much later, when everyone had gone and the guests were in their rooms and Mevrouw van Germert sitting in her drawing room doing tapestry work to settle her before she went to bed too, that Annis and Jake found themselves alone in the hall.

'Come in here,' he said, and opened the door into the small sitting room at the end of the passage. 'I've hardly seen you.' He stood and looked at her in a leisurely fashion. 'I like that dress too. Is it new?'

It was a printed silk, with a scooped-out neckline, a tiny waist and a full skirt, and it became her very well. 'Yes—it seemed something of an occasion ...'

He swung close to her. 'Indeed it is. Are you scared?'

'No. Are you?'

He shook his head. 'No—only that I'll trip up going into the Raadhuis and fall flat on my face.'

She laughed and he said gently: 'That's better.' He put a hand in his pocket. 'I've a present for you, I hope you'll wear it tomorrow.'

The case was long and leather-covered and Annis opened it slowly. There was a string of pearls inside with a diamond and sapphire clasp. 'They're gorgeous!' she whispered. 'Of couse I'll wear them. Oh, Jake, thank you.' She ran a finger along their milky richness. 'I've never had anything as lovely.'

She reached up and kissed him a little shyly, wishing that he would fling down his crutches and put his arms round her and kiss her too. But he didn't. 'You must go to bed, my dear,' he observed mildly. 'Tomorrow is going to be a long day.'

CHAPTER SEVEN

THE wedding morning was bright and clear with a blue sky and sunshine tempered by a chilly little wind. Annis, awake early and hanging out of her window, sniffed at the pleasant garden smells and leaned out a little further so that she could see the magnificent roses climbing the end wall—New Dawn, pale pink and still prolific although summer was dying. A small sound below her made her look down. Jake was there, in slacks and a sweater, leaning on his crutches, and she gazed at him open-mouthed. 'What on earth ...' she began.

'Hullo, Annis. How about a stroll before breakfast? Cor's in the car with some coffee, and so is Mike.' He grinned suddenly. 'And put something on, my dear.'

Annis withdrew rapidly, thinking vexedly as she did so that it was a pity that all her prettiest nighties were packed and she was wearing a cotton one with very little top to it. 'All right,' she hissed, 'I'll be down— I didn't expect you ...'

'I should hope not,' said Jake.

She joined him presently, wearing slacks and a blouse and with her fiery hair loose. She had washed her face after a fashion and she looked about twelve years old. Perhaps that was why Jake didn't kiss her. They went round the side of the house to where Cor sat in the Bristol and he wished her good morning before pouring coffee for them both.

'Have some yourself, Cor,' said Jake. 'You deserve it, being got out of your bed at this hour. Only another week or two, then I can drive myself.'

They sipped their coffee in companionable silence before Jake said: 'Now a little stroll, don't you think, Annis?'

She nodded. 'It's a bit funny,' she began, 'I mean, in a couple of hours' time I'll be getting into wedding finery. I wish it was all over, Jake.'

He smiled at her as they started off with Mike walking sedately beside them.

'I think you'll enjoy it, my dear, once it actually starts.' He stopped to examine a bed of roses. 'Mind you're ready for me when I come.'

She gave him a quick glance. 'I promise that. How long will it all last?'

'The reception? Oh, about nine o'clock this evening, I should think, perhaps a little later. We shall have supper by ourselves, I'm sorry it's not longer. Once I've got this damn plaster off, we'll go away for a bit, if you like.'

'Only if it doesn't upset your work. I shall be happy in Goes, Jake.'

'You love the house, don't you? That's more than half the battle ...'

They were coming back towards the house. She stopped suddenly. 'What do you mean? What battle?'

He stared at her for a long moment. 'Forgetting is always a battle.'

Here was the chance to tell him, and it couldn't be on a better day. 'Jake, there's something ...'

She was interrupted by Great-Aunt Mary's voice
from her bedroom window. It was full of shocked
horror. 'Annis, what do you think you're doing? Don't
you know that the pair of you aren't supposed to see
each other until the wedding? I've never heard of anything like it! Come in at once, you're supposed to be
having breakfast in bed.'

Jake laughed. 'My fault,' he called, and then turned
to Annis. 'Go back to bed, my dear, and make everyone happy. I'll be along later.' He paused. 'Whatever
it was you were going to tell me will have to wait. Or
was it important?'

Annis sighed soundlessly. That was the second time
she'd been thwarted; could it be unkind Fate or just
bad luck? 'Not a bit important,' she told him lightly.

'And don't you dare kiss her,' called Great-Aunt
Mary, still watching.

'I never could resist a challenge,' said Jake, and bent
over her. She supposed it was because Great-Aunt Mary
was watching that he kissed her so slowly.

She was ready far too soon. She took a last look at
her reflection, decided that the cream organza was
really rather dreamy, pulled the little coronet of white
flowers straight on the top of her piled-up hair, and
went downstairs. Her aunt, Carol and Freddy were
on the point of leaving in Freddy's car, for he had
arrived to drive them to the Raadhuis, his rakish Jag
followed by Hans driving the BMW with Mevrouw
van Germert sitting in the back. She looked stately and
very handsome in her steel-grey dress and feathered
hat, but her face had softened as she kissed Annis before she went. 'Jake won't keep you waiting, my dear,

just sit quietly in the drawing room.'

So she sat, thinking that it was a funny way to get married. At home Freddy would have been waiting with her and she wouldn't have seen Jake until she was actually in the church. She wondered what they would say to each other when he arrived.

He came into the room so quietly that she didn't hear the soft thud of his crutches on the carpet. His: 'Oh, very nice, very nice indeed,' brought her to her startled feet with a loud gasp.

'My goodness, you made me jump!' she told him.

'If it comes to that, you made me jump too. Very beautiful, dear Annis.'

He looked pretty good himself. The plaster was concealed in his pinstriped trouser leg—she supposed it had a zip somewhere; his tail-coat fitted him perfectly, his grey tie exactly matched the grey of the top hat he held in his hand. She said 'Thank you, Jake,' and added: 'You look pretty good, too.' She went to meet him across the lovely room. 'Is your leg all right?'

'Couldn't be better.' He bent and kissed her cheek. 'Feeling better about it all now?'

'Yes. Everything's fine, Jake.' She put out a hand and touched his coat sleeve. 'Jake, I'll be a good wife to you—I know that sounds old-fashioned, but I mean it.'

'If I didn't have these blasted crutches to wrestle with, I'd show you my appreciation for those words. I know you'll be a good wife, darling Annis. I intend to be a good husband.' His voice was light and she

couldn't see his eyes as he had dropped their lids.
'Shall we go?'

The Bristol had been decked with flowers, the back
window was framed with them, there was a garland
at each side and Cor had an enormous nosegay in his
buttonhole. He opened the door for them and Jake
leaned forward and took her bouquet from the back
seat. A lovely shower of cream roses and orange blossom
and white orchids. He gave it to her with a little bow
and then kissed her briefly while the entire staff of his
mother's house, watching from the porch, clapped
loudly. Annis remembered to turn and wave before
she got into the car.

There was quite a crowd in the market square before the Raadhuis. They went up the steps slowly to
where the great door stood open and Annis longed to
take Jake's arm because it all seemed so strange. But
he needed both hands to get himself and his crutches
up to the door, so she clutched her bouquet and
smiled shyly at the upturned faces.

Once inside, they were led to the Wedding Chamber,
to pause in the small anteroom so that Carol could
join them with Freddy, before the double doors were
opened and they went in. The room was a large, lofty
one with rows of little velvet-covered chairs facing a
carved table behind which the Burgermeester stood,
ready to marry them. There seemed to be at least twice
as many people there as she had expected and almost
all of them were strangers. They paused inside the
doorway and Jake leaned on his crutches and took her
hand in his; only for a moment, but it reassured her.
She lifted her chin, smiled at him, and walked beside

him to the table and sat down beside him in front of it.

The ceremony was brief and she wasn't sure that she felt married when it was over; she signed her name and watched a great many other people do the same before they walked back the way they had come, down the steps and into the car once more. There were more people now and someone taking photos. None of it seemed quite real. The drive to the church was brief, for its great bulk overshadowed the Raadhuis from a nearby square. It could have been even briefer, but so that all the guests could get there first, Cor took the car on a short drive through the town, to return to the church once the last guest had gone in. And this time Annis did feel married. She didn't understand the service, but the form of it was similar to her own church, and Jake had explained it to her earlier; even the hymn tunes were the same and the church was beautiful, its magnificent organ echoing out in its vast interior. The ring was put on her finger for a second time, a plain gold band exactly matching the one she had got for Jake, and she touched it briefly as they started down the aisle. Now she really was Jake's wife and even though the future might hold a few pitfalls and the uncertainty that he might never love her as she loved him, she was happy.

There was another small crowd waiting outside the church and more photographs before they got into the Bristol again and were driven away to Jake's house. The staff were lined up outside, waiting for them and they had to stop and shake everyone by the hand before they went inside. At the door Jake said half laughing: 'I'm supposed to carry you over the threshold, aren't I? but I don't think I can; something else which will have to be put off until I've got this plaster off. This will do instead, perhaps.'

He kissed her and took no notice at all of the murmur of approval from those watching, then, with her beside him, he went into the house.

The reception was to be in the drawing room, its furniture moved back against its walls, small tables and chairs in their place. At one end there was a long table where they were to sit with the closer members of the family. It sparkled with silver and glass and exquisitely arranged flowers, but there was no time to examine it. Jake caught her hand in his. 'Here they come,' he said as the door opened and his mother, escorted by an uncle whose name Annis couldn't remember, came in, then Great-Aunt Mary, almost unrecognisable in a feather toque and an elegant two-piece. She had another uncle in tow, a merry old man whom Jake had introduced as Oom Karel, and behind them came Carol and Freddy, obviously enjoying each other's company. There was barely time to exchange kisses and handshakes before the guests streamed in. And after that it was a confused muddle of wedding hats, curious eyes, hearty gentlemen who beat Jake remorselessly on the shoulders and kissed her with gusto and cheerful younger faces, who eyed her with friendliness and told her how pretty she looked. Then she heard Jake say: 'Ah, Waldo and Olympia,' and met the dark eyes of a very pretty girl with a quantity of hair piled into a knot at the back of her neck and crowned by a little flowery hat. She smiled widely at Annis and offered a hand, and Jake went on: 'Two friends of mine, and now they're friends of ours, my dear. They live in Middelburg, remember, and have a clutch of children.'

Olympia laughed and put up her face to be kissed while her husband leaned down to kiss Annis's cheek. 'Just as pretty as he said you were and a good deal prettier,' he told her. He was as tall as Jake and just as large and smiled at her in such a friendly fashion that she found herself smiling back, aware that here were indeed two friends. 'We'll see you later,' murmured Olympia, and moved away to make room for an elderly, cross-looking lady, dressed well but in a very old-fashioned style and wearing a great many diamond rings.

'Tante Wilhelmina, how delightful,' observed Jake. 'My wife, Annis.'

The old lady stared at her from small bright blue eyes. 'H'm— pretty enough, and got some flesh on her bones, I'm glad to see. Give me a kiss, my girl, you may call me Tante Wilhelmina as well.'

She swept on and Annis whispered: 'Which side of your family is she? She's a bit overpowering.'

Jake chuckled. 'A great-aunt on my father's side. She's a baroness and very, very rich. She lives in den Haag all alone except for the servants, her daughters are married and live in America, and her son married a girl she doesn't like. I don't like her either. Here they come now.'

He leaned on his crutches and tucked a hand under her arm and gave it a reassuring squeeze. Annis knew at once why he didn't like the youngish woman standing before them; she was good-looking, but her eyes were hard and searching and her mouth had turned down corners. She was very well dressed but without much taste, and when she spoke her voice was high and faintly querulous. 'So this is the bride. I must say, Jake, I'm surprised that you've married a foreigner. I quite thought you'd settle for Nina ...' She gave a spiteful little laugh. 'Perhaps she wouldn't have you.' She shook Annis's hand, her eyes on the pearls round her throat. 'You've got the pearls already, I see.'

Annis smiled politely. The woman was ghastly, but she supposed there was one in every family. She listened to Jake making polite conversation with her as she shook hands with her husband, a man a good deal older than his wife with a florid face and a roving eye. Jake was equally polite to him as well and when they had disappeared into the throng of guests, turned to Annis and winked at her. 'There can't be many more,' he told her softly. 'We've earned our champagne.'

'Who's Nina?' asked Annis. Her face was calm and smiling, but her green eyes looked greener than ever.

Jake laughed. 'Ah—well, I'll tell you about her some time.' He said smoothly: 'And here are the last of the stragglers ...' He turned to greet two elderly, comfortably plump ladies, who smiled and twinkled at Annis as they kissed her warmly. It was a pity that they spoke in Dutch because she had to rely on Jake translating what they said and he had obviously given her a shortened version, but all the same, they exuded kindness, chattering away like two elderly magpies.

'Two aunts on Mother's side, Tante Beatrix and Tante Coralie. Both nice.' He smiled down at her. 'We had better join the others.'

The next hour was rather dreamlike. Annis nibbled at the delicious bits and pieces offered her, drank a little too much champagne and listened to a variety of speeches, all of them delivered in English in her honour, although sometimes they were a little difficult to follow. And presently the tables were cleared away and she and Jake walked among their guests and this time she remembered at least some of their names, and when she didn't, Jake was there to prompt her quietly. The evening was well advanced when the first of the guests began to leave; Annis, quite tired by now and rather hungry because she had really eaten very little and drunk too much, shook hands all over again and proffered her cheek to countless aunts and uncles and cousins. Her own guests were going back to an hotel for the night and she said goodbye to them too, then found a quiet corner so that she might have a last word with her aunt and Freddy and Carol.

'Marvellous!' exclaimed Carol. 'You look so beautiful, Annis, and what a lovely wedding—and how romantic, Jake going to fetch you with a bouquet. I suppose he hasn't got a brother?'

Freddy threw a proprietorial arm round her pink-clad shoulders. 'You don't need to look further,' he observed lightly. 'I'm his brother-in-law now, and that's near enough for you, darling.'

Carol had pinkened a little and not answered, and Annis had laughed at them as though it were a joke, although she wasn't sure that it was. It would be nice ... She caught Great-Aunt Mary's eye, saw the decided twinkle in it and bent forward and gave that lady an affectionate kiss. 'I'll come over and see you soon,' she promised, and pinkened in her turn at her aunt's brisk:

'And Jake will come with you, naturally.'

'And what will Jake do naturally?' His voice made them all start a little.

'Come and visit me, dear boy, both of you.' She chuckled. 'Although after seeing this enormous house of yours I hardly dare ask you.'

He planted a kiss on her cheek. 'They're both homes —size hasn't anything to do with it. Of course we'll come. We're not going away, you know—I can't spare the time, so we'll have a holiday in a little while. In any case I'm rather hampered with these.' He thumped his crutches on the floor. 'You're all going back with Mama, of course.'

They all went into the hall where Mevrouw van Germert joined them presently, to be driven away by the stolid Hans. The great house seemed very quiet after that and it was Jake who broke the silence. 'You look beautiful,' he observed, 'but how about getting into something easy and we'll have supper. Will half an hour suit you?'

Annis went upstairs with Katrina the housekeeper leading the way and this time she was shown into another bedroom, an enormous apartment overlooking the street, its two windows hung with pale brocade, a fourposter bed, covered with the same rich stuff, against the opposite wall. There was a massive tallboy flanked by two velvet-covered chairs along one side and the fourth wall held three doors. Annis, left alone by the smiling Katrina, skimmed round the room, examining everything and liking it all very much. Finally she opened the doors. A bathroom, fitted out in a misty blue with piles of coloured towels on its shelves, a great cupboard which lighted up as she opened its door, revealing rows of shelves and lines of padded hangers with her clothes already neatly arranged, and lastly a short passage with a door at its end. It led to another bedroom, much smaller but equally comfortable and obviously in use. Jake's—she shut the door quickly and wondered what she would have done if he had been there, then instantly told herself she was a fool; she was his wife now, even though she hadn't got used to the idea.

She took off her veil and sat down on the bed. It had been an exciting, unforgettable day and she was deeply grateful to Jake because he had shown her off with such pride to his enormous family. At least he had a fondness for her and her first idea that he had wanted to marry her so that he might have someone to run his house hadn't been in the least bit true. Katrina did that beautifully, although she could quite see that with a family and friends in such numbers a wife to arrange his entertaining and social life would be of great help to him; she didn't think he was a man to worry about such things, merely expecting them to be arranged for him. She got out of her dress slowly and went to run a bath. And who was Nina? Somone important or merely a name dropped in spite by that beastly woman with the cold eyes? Annis lay in the bath until the water cooled and then raced through her dressing because she had already been more than half an hour. She put on a simple little printed dress with a high neck and elbow sleeves gathered into bands, brushed her hair back and let it hang down her back, and went downstairs.

Jake was leaning against the massive post at the foot of the staircase. 'Hullo—I was beginning to wonder if you'd flown out of a window.'

She beamed at him, suddenly very happy; he looked splendid despite the crutches, his grey suit exactly right for the occasion, and as well as that he looked content so that his rather arrogant face had softened. And there was nothing wrong with the admiring look he had given her. They went in to supper and Annis, sitting opposite him at the big mahogany table, thought how nice it was to feel so completely at ease with someone, especially when he was her husband. Cor waited on them, beaming goodwill as he served hors d'oeuvres, fillet of beef Meurice, and followed these with a magnificent mouthwatering confection which he assured them with pride had been specially thought up by the cook, a wonderful concoction of fresh fruit in brandy, ice cream, tiny macaroons and almonds, the whole wreathed around with whipped cream. Annis, who hadn't eaten much at the reception, enjoyed it all and over a second helping asked if they might not thank the cook. 'All this on top of the reception. They must have worked in the kitchen for hours, only you'll have to do it, Jake, because they won't understand me.'

So the cook, Minna, and her two kitchen helpers were sent for and Jake made a short speech, not a word of which did Annis understand, but at the end she said 'Thank you' and smiled widely at them and when they had gone she said urgently: 'Jake, I must learn

Dutch—how long will it take?'

He grinned at her cheerfully. 'It's not an easy language, but I'll find someone to teach you the basics of conversation; the grammar can be wrestled with later. Shall we have coffee in the drawing room?'

They talked for a bit, about the wedding and the various people at it, and Jake told her a little of his family. There seemed so many of them, she observed, bewildered by the names. 'But you'll not see much of them,' he pointed out. 'Which reminds me—Waldo and Olympia have asked us to go over to Middleburg for dinner one evening. You'd like that, wouldn't you?'

Annis nodded. 'I liked them. Jake, what time do we have breakfast—will someone call me?'

'Yes, of course, but you don't have to get up unless you want to. I breakfast at half past seven, take Mike for a walk and go to the surgery at eight-thirty. Rather early, perhaps?'

'I'm used to getting up early. Besides, we shan't see much of each other otherwise.' She went pink under his little smile and the awful thought that perhaps he didn't want to see all that much of her crossed her mind.

'I expect you're used to being on your own,' she said gruffly. 'Your post and the papers ...'

'Yes, I am, but I'd much rather have you to keep me company, as you say we shan't see a great deal of each other.' He put down his coffee cup and sat staring at her. 'Only another week or two and I'll be rid of this plaster, which will rather alter things.' He added abruptly: 'You're happy, Annis?'

She looked down at her hands. 'Yes, Jake, I am.'

'Getting over Ola? It takes time, my dear.' He sounded so sympathetic that she wanted to tell him how wrong he was about it all, but he went on easily: 'You won't have much time to sit and remember, and that should be a good thing. Katrina is longing to lead you round the house and show you everything; she'll help you with the household shopping and Cor will translate for you until you can manage for yourself. He keeps the accounts too, but perhaps you would like to see how everything is managed. We'll go into finances one day soon; there's an account for the house expenses and I've arranged for you to have your own account. Your allowance is already in it—every quarter, if that suits you? Don't worry if you spend too much, I have enough money—more than enough.'

Annis said, 'Yes, Jake,' meekly and became silent again; the moment had passed and she wondered when she would have a chance to tell him, or if that chance would ever occur, for that matter. Certainly not then and now, for he added firmly: 'I expect you're tired.' Suddenly he sounded very formal, just as though he were addressing one of his patients. 'I hope you'll be comfortable. Don't hesitate to ask for anything you want—this is your home now.'

He had got to his feet and was leaning on his crutches and she had the feeling that she had been dismissed, kindly and politely, but dismissed. A little bubble of despondency exploded inside her so that she spoke snappily:

'I'm sure there's everything I could possibly need, thank you. Goodnight, Jake.'

She rushed to the door and was through it before he

could get half way across the room. Somehow she held
back her tears until she reached her room. Tears of
temper, she assured herself, because he hadn't even
bothered to wish her goodnight. Why had she married
him? she demanded crossly of the beautiful room
around her, and then wailed: 'Oh, I love him, don't
I? And I've been beastly ... that lovely reception and
the flowers and my pearls and meeting all his family,
and I expect he's just as fed up about his wretched
plaster as I am.' She started to undress and then half
way through tore into her dressing gown and ran
downstairs again. She couldn't go to bed without telling him she was sorry for being so thoroughly beastly
... She opened the door and nipped across the room
before he could get out of his chair and flung herself
down on her knees beside him. 'Jake, I'm so sorry! I
was rude and horrible—after all you've done for me—
my lovely wedding day and this simply wonderful
house and the pearls—and I had to snap at you like
that. I'm an ungrateful wretch.'

He was sitting very straight in his chair, looking at
her, holding one of her hands. 'Now there's a nice
girl,' he said, and it hurt her that he should look
amused as he said it. 'But you're making a mountain
out of a molehill, you know. I hadn't noticed you
being—er—ungrateful. You're upsetting yourself for
no reason at all, my dear. You're more tired than you
realise.'

She stared back at him. He looked and sounded remote now and she went hot with embarrassment. He
must think her a fool, trying to draw attention to herself. She jumped to her feet. 'Well, yes, I think I am.

Thank you for my—our lovely wedding day. Good-night, Jake.'

She didn't look at him but went as quickly as she could from the room. To burst into tears on her wedding day wouldn't do at all; that was a luxury she would allow herself presently. But once in her enormous bed, sitting up high against the lace-trimmed pillows, there seemed no point in howling her eyes out over something which after all was exactly what she had expected. Besides, it was a waste of time to cry. She put her chin on her knees and clasped her arms round them and thought long and hard. She had known that Jake didn't love her—not in the way she loved him, at any rate, but there was no reason why he shouldn't—in time. She would have to discover what kind of girl he liked and model herself along those lines. She would have to discover too his likes and dislikes and which of his friends he liked to see most; the clothes he preferred her to wear ... and she would have to learn Dutch just as quickly as possible. It was really quite a programme, and she must try and get through it before he had his plaster off, for he had said that then they would go on holiday, and what better chance to further her purpose?

She got out of bed and took a look at herself in the pier glass, peering anxiously into her pretty face, searching for lines and wrinkles. There weren't any, nor were there any grey hairs in her glorious tumbling mop, and there was nothing wrong with her figure, a bit too opulent for the fashionable, perhaps, but she supposed she passed muster. She got back into bed, and in the middle of her plans, went to sleep.

She woke to find the sun streaming through the windows and Ellie standing by the bed with a tray. She smiled and said something in Dutch, and Annis said 'Goeden morgen,' and hoped there would be no need for her to try and say anything else. There wasn't; there was an envelope on the tray, addressed to her in Jake's spidery hand. 'I told Cor to let you sleep until nine o'clock,' it said, 'later if you want to. I'll be home at lunch time and Mevrouw Pette will be calling about eleven o'clock to discuss your Dutch lessons.' He had signed it simply: Jake.

Annis ate her breakfast quickly and then lay in a hot bath trying to decide what to wear. The days were growing cooler but the sun still shone; she chose a dress, a slim cotton jersey with a little jacket, and because she was Mevrouw van Germert now, she did her hair in a coil, smoothing it into wings on either side, from which small curls escaped almost immediately. She did her face carefully and then sat practising a variety of expressions in the looking glass. She was a little put out that she hadn't been called in time to have breakfast with Jake—she had understood that that was the arrangement, but perhaps he had really wanted her to have her sleep out, and not, as a nasty little voice at the back of her head kept whispering, because he hadn't wanted her at breakfast to spoil his solitude. She must remember to smile and look composed, and not frown, she told herself as she went down the staircase and into the hall, where Cor, appearing silently, wished her a dignified good morning and led her to the library, a room, he volunteered, which seemed suitable for the giving of lessons.

'And I will bring coffee at once, Mevrouw,' he promised, vanishing as silently as he had arrived.

The library was rather dark, by reason of the great number of books lining its walls and the two narrow windows at one end of it. There was a narrow gallery running round two sides of it with a few steps to it and Annis prowled round, peering at titles in German, Dutch and English. Most of them looked learned and she was glad to see that laid out on the round table in the centre of the room were an assortment of magazines, both Dutch and English. She picked up *Harpers* and retired to a large leather armchair to browse, feeling a little guilty because she wasn't doing anything useful. Indeed, when Cor came presently with the coffee she asked him: 'Ought I to see Katrina or something, Cor? I know she runs the house beautifully, but I'll have to learn, won't I?'

He gave her a fatherly smile. 'The doctor suggested that you should do nothing this morning, Mevrouw, except meet Mevrouw Pette. He will be home to lunch and Katrina has arranged a simple meal for you both. Perhaps after lunch you might like to come to the kitchen and discuss the evening menu with Katrina. I will be there, of course, to assist you.'

Annis nodded. 'I'd like that. Will you show Mevrouw Pette in when she comes, Cor? And should she have coffee too?'

'I shall bring a fresh tray, Mevrouw.'

After he had gone, she picked up *Harpers* again and sipped her coffee. She would have to get used to Jake's way of living; not at all like her own had been. She had a fleeting memory of morning coffee at the hospital,

drunk in a tearing hurry between jobs, and on Spitzbergen she had mostly had hers out of doors. She
sighed. Life had been simple there, although perhaps
Ola had complicated it just for a time. She drank
another cup and studied the fashions. The prices were
shocking although some of the clothes were absolutely
wonderful. The thought struck her that if she wanted
to, she could have them if she wished; Jake had given
her an allowance which would allow for extravagance
if she were so inclined. She was weighing the advan-
tages of a soft wool two-piece against a coat-dress when
Cor came in and announced Mevrouw Pette, and
Annis got to her feet.

She had imagined that her teacher would be a
serious woman, rather elderly, wearing glasses and flat
shoes and fearfully keen on grammar, but she saw at
once that her imagination had run away with her.
Mevrouw Pette was young, stylish and pretty, with a
pleasant smiling face and a brisk voice.

They shook hands and eyed each other while they sat
down. Annis smiled suddenly. 'I don't know why, but
I thought you'd be elderly and stern.'

Mevrouw Pette giggled. 'I am none of these things,
Mevrouw van Germert. I will tell you that I am a
widow, my husband was a patient of the doctor's and
he has been so kind as to encourage me to give English people here Dutch lessons; that is five years ago
now, and I have many pupils, thanks to him, and now
I hope I am to have you too.'

'Oh, please. I want to learn to speak Dutch just as
quickly as I can.'

'Then we will work hard. My mother was English,

but I went to school in Holland, although we always spoke English at home. It annoyed me then, but now I am glad of it.' She paused while Cor came in with more coffee. 'You are just married?' she asked when he had gone. 'You do not know Goes?'

'Well, a little, I'll find my way around. Shall I need any books?'

Mevrouw Pette nodded. 'I will give you a list, and now if you would like it, we will talk about your lessons. If you would tell me when you would like me to come?'

The two of them put their heads together and before Mevrouw Pette got up to go it had been decided that Annis was to have a lesson three times a week in the mornings, and on the other days work at her books. 'We shall work hard,' Mevrouw Pette promised her. 'We will surprise the good doctor; each week something.' She beamed satisfaction at Annis and made her say goodbye in Dutch by way of a beginning.

Annis found herself settling into her new life with astonishing ease; she had had her doubts about doing nothing at all, but she found that her days were filled with a multitude of occupations, most of them very much to her liking. Breakfast, she quickly discovered, was a meal which Jake liked to eat more or less in silence; he had his post to open, the headlines of the papers to read, and more often than not, his pocket-book open beside him in which to scribble notes. Annis, after one such meal with him, relieved him of the chore of opening the letters, kept his coffee cup filled and beyond a cheerful good morning only spoke when she was spoken to, and was rewarded for this by his: 'What a restful girl you are, Annis,' as he eyed her over his letters. 'And nice to look at too, I can see that breakfast will no longer be a necessary chore before I start work.'

She had found nothing to say to that, although she had gone rather pink.

Her mornings were filled; a painstaking inspection of the store cupboards with Katrina, doing her best to repeat the Dutch names for the things in them, then a laborious reading of the menus for lunch and dinner followed by a quick dash round the garden with Mike before going to the small sitting room ready for Mevrouw Pette, and when that lady didn't come, to the library where she sat at a desk in a businesslike fashion, worrying at her Dutch books like a dog with a bone. Sometimes, when Jake came home for lunch, she tried out a few words of Dutch on him, a little nervous of being laughed at, a thing which he never did, encouraging her to talk, helping her.

They had been married for five days and it was Sunday on the following day. Jake had been out of the house most of the day, but now, over a late dinner, he observed: 'You've been pretty marvellous; not a grumble or a frown from you since we married, and heaven knows it must have been dull for you at least some of the time. Thank you, my dear. Things will be easier next week, we might even have a trip to den Haag and go round the shops. And tomorrow I shall be free all day. Would you like a trip somewhere?'

Annis smiled widely. Her five days of forbearance had paid off. 'Well, it would be fun, but you don't like not driving, do you?'

'Hate it, but I've not much choice for the moment. The plaster's coming off next week, by the way, and they'll put on a walking iron for another week or two. Just as soon as it's possible they'll take that off and I'll be able to manage with a stick.' He stared at her hard. 'You really don't mind if we don't use the car? What would you like to do?'

She hesitated. 'I think it would be lovely to go round the house with you and you can tell me everything there is to know about it—only would that bore you?'

'Not in the least—and how about dining at Schudderbeurs?'

'Lovely. When will you get a day off?'

'Wednesday. You'd like to go shopping?'

'I've no need to buy anything,' began Annis. His laugh interrupted her. 'I'm sure you'll see something.' His face became serious. 'You're happy, Annis?' And after a pause: 'No regrets?'

'None, Jake, and I'm very happy.' It was a pity that there was the length of the table between them, as it was hardly conducive to an intimate conversation. Perhaps it would be easier in the drawing room. 'Shall we have our coffee?' she suggested, and once seated there with the coffee tray before her and Jake lounging in his great chair opposite, she drew a deep breath, ready to say all the things she had been longing to say. Only she didn't get the chance. The door opened and Cor came in.

'Mijnheer en Mevrouw van Tigler,' he announced in a voice which held discreet disapproval. And 'Oh, God,' said Jake under his breath, 'at this hour too!'

He got to his feet as the woman who had asked about Nina at the wedding surged into the room, her husband behind her. She was in evening dress and her one swift glance in Annis's direction took in the simple jersey dress she was wearing and despised it even while she exclaimed with calculated sweetness: 'Jake, my dear, and Annis—we're on our way back from Utrecht—the Burgermeester's reception, you know, and I told Wim that we simply had to come and see you both and have a drink with you.' Her eye fell on the coffee tray. 'Oh, coffee—have you only just dined?'

Jake replied with cold civility, greeted Wim and turned to Annis with a smile. 'We were going to have an early night,' he observed, 'but do stay for a drink. What will you have?'

'Whisky.' Mevrouw van Tigler sat down beside Annis. 'Annis, how nice to have a little chat with you; there was no chance at the wedding. I expect you have had a wonderful week.'

'If you mean have we been out and about each day,' said Annis calmly, 'we haven't, but just being together is enough, Mervrouw van Tigler.'

Her companion's beringed hand rested on her arm. 'Call me Ria,' she smiled brilliantly. 'After all, you're family now.'

She accepted a glass from Jake and waited while he went to sit by her husband. Too far away for help, thought Annis vexedly, unless he had the power to hear over and above the normal. Apparently he had, for when Ria asked: 'And has Jake told you all about his past life?—quite worth hearing, I can assure you—though you'll know all about it, I daresay.'

Annis picked up her coffee cup and took a sip, wondering what to say. Whatever she said this horrible woman was going to turn and twist it ...

'You always were a woman for asking questions and wanting the answers, Ria.' He added: 'Is that why you came?' He looked at his watch. 'It's very late.'

Ria flushed angrily. 'You haven't changed, Jake—still rude when it suits you. I suppose you want Annis to think you never looked at another girl before she married you.'

It seemed time to join in. 'I certainly wouldn't have married him if he hadn't,' said Annis sweetly. Her heart gave a happy little leap at the look of approval which Jake sent her. 'And it's a pity it's so late—Jake's had a busy day.'

'You must have known you wouldn't be able to see much of him,' said Ria snappily. 'A doctor ...'

'Well, of course I did; having been a nurse in hospital you know, one quickly realised that doctors can't call their days their own. But Jake's doing a job he likes, a useful job, too. To do nothing at all must be so boring for a man.'

She could almost hear the silence which greeted this remark and when she looked across at Wim it was to see that his ruddy complexion had turned a rich claret and he was looking annoyed. There was no expression on Jake's face at all, though, and she didn't have time to look very well because Ria had finished her whisky and got to her feet. She said with artificial sweetness: 'You must come and see us soon, both of you.' She went to the door with Annis beside her and paused there. 'You're such a lucky man, Jake,' she said loudly, 'to have found someone so—so suitable after Nina.'

Annis felt his arm round her shoulders and because he was leaning on his other crutch, it was extremely heavy. 'I'm a very lucky man,' he agreed affably. 'Annis is, as you say, so suitable.' He left Annis and opened the door, and then swung across the hall to wait while Cor let his visitors out.

Annis, alone in the lovely room, wandered across to the sofa where she had been sitting. Ria was a nasty piece of work and she had succeeded in spoiling their evening, at least her evening. It was impossible to see what Jake thought about it, for his face looked very much as usual, a little austere and arrogant but calm enough. He wasn't a man to show his feelings.

As soon as he was back in the room she asked: 'Why am I suitable, Jake?' And as she said it she knew that it was hopeless to get a reply from him. He said amicably enough: 'The reasons are obvious, my dear. You're a nurse, you're beautiful, you're a delightful companion.' He smiled at her, but she knew that he was angry. It was foolish of her to persist with:

'And Nina—was she suitable too?'

He stood leaning on his crutches. 'You don't have to worry about Nina, my dear. Ria was being spiteful, more so than usual because you see Wim does nothing at all; he hasn't lifted a finger since the day he was born, that's why he's such a dull devil.' He added: 'Go to bed, Annis, and don't turn your molehill into a mountain.' She felt his light kiss on her cheek as she went.

CHAPTER EIGHT

ANNIS went down to breakfast the next morning looking a little pale and heavy-eyed; not because she had
been crying, that would have been useless and a waste
of time, she had told herself as she had sped upstairs
with a barely audible goodnight for Jake. No, she had
a good deal to think about. Nina was becoming a
nuisance and a threat to her peace of mind—besides,
she was important enough to Jake for him to refuse to
talk about her. Somehow she would have to find out
more about the other girl, and she had spent a large
part of the night cudgelling her brains as to how best
to do that. She could of course ask her mother-in-law,
but it seemed unlikely that that formidable lady, however well disposed towards her, would tell tales about
her son, and it was impossible, though tempting, to
ask Cor. That left her with Jake's sister, whom she didn't
know well and who had gone away on holiday anyway,
and Olympia van der Graaf. The latter, she had decided before closing her eyes and sleeping for the small
slice of the night which was left.

Jake was already in the small pleasant breakfast
room, standing at the window looking out into the
street with Mike beside him. He greeted her cheerfully
and although his dark eyes swept over her tired face
with swift intentness, he merely remarked upon the
dismal weather outside, giving the opinion that he was

glad that they would be indoors for most of the day.

'We really must have a talk,' he observed as they sat down and she lifted the coffee pot to pour their coffee. 'What about?'

'Money mostly, boring to you, but you'll have to know something of our financial affairs ... and holidays, too. What would you like to do? Travel a little —go to England? Cruise?'

She buttered a roll and popped a piece into her mouth. 'And when will that be?'

'October—the end of October, I'm afraid. Not too far away to make plans.' He began to discuss what they might do and she answered him pleasantly and thought about Nina while her insides melted at the sight of him sitting on the other side of the table.

'You're not listening,' said Jake.

''Oh, yes, I—well, actually perhaps I wasn't. I was thinking; it's—it's funny, sitting here with you, I mean being your wife ...' She saw his eyebrows lift and hastened to add: 'Not funny—strange, unlikely.'

Jake gave her a long hard stare. 'I think I prefer funny.' He spoke so coldly that she said, suddenly fierce:

'You know very well what I mean.'

He grinned at her with faint mockery. 'You're very beautiful when you're cross.'

'I am not cross.'

'No? But still beautiful.' He smiled at her, with no mockery this time, and she caught her breath; for the moment the vexed question of Nina could wait.

They spent the entire morning going round the house, not just looking at the rooms, but examining the treasures in them, while Jake patiently told her the history of each piece of silver, each picture, each chair and chest and cabinet, and she found it enthralling. They were in the little garden room when Cor tracked them down with the coffee tray and they stayed there to drink it. Annis, mulling over all the titbits of information she had gathered about the old house, poured it from the little silver coffee pot and handed Jake a cup. As he took it from her, he observed with pleasure: 'This is nice, just the two of us.'

She smiled widely. 'Yes, isn't it? But don't you miss Spitzbergen?'

'Yes, but my home and my work are here. But we'll go back there one day if you would like that—but perhaps you wouldn't want to do that.' He gave her a quick glance and hoisted his plastered leg over a chair. 'Does Freddy intend to go back?'

'I don't know. He seldom tells anyone what he intends doing next.'

'He and your bridesmaid were getting on very well.'

'Yes. Wouldn't it be lovely if ... I'd like him to settle down.' She refilled his cup. 'But perhaps he's a little too young to settle down ...'

'Isn't it a question of finding the right girl rather than his age?' Jake asked idly.

Annis wanted above all things to ask him if he had found the right girl, but when she looked at him she saw that he was smiling faintly, waiting for her to say something. His eyes looked black, without expression, and she looked away quickly. 'More coffee?' she asked him, and didn't see his faint frown.

They resumed their inspection presently, wandering

in and out of the small rooms on the second and third floors, until Annis, on her own now because Jake couldn't manage the steep little stairs, climbed them to the attics. They were big rooms, low-ceilinged and with great windows, each with a pulley above it so that furniture might be moved in and out of the house easily. One was filled with old trunks, cricket bats, bundles of ice skates and odds and ends of furniture, and its walls were hung with rugger boots on hooks, a couple of children's sleds and a miscellaneous collection of out-of-date raincoats, woollen scarves and old hats. The second room was rather a surprise—a games room, with a train set occupying the whole of one end of the floor, a table tennis table by the window and a billiard table, rather the worse for wear, and round the wall shelves filled with model boats, boxes of games and a vast collection of balls and tennis rackets.

When she got back to where Jake was waiting for her she asked: 'Was that your playroom in the attic?'

He nodded, smiling. 'Yes, my very own room, even Elsa only came when she was invited. The nursery's on the first floor—I'll show you.'

It was through a small archway and down a narrow passage. A large airy room, empty save for a large dolls' house on a table against one wall and a glass-fronted cupboard in which rows of dolls were neatly arranged. Annis would have liked to have examined them more closely, but Jake said briskly: 'Not much here to look at—come downstairs. I'll show you the family Bible.' After lunch he ushered her into his study, a small booklined room opening out from the hall at the opposite end to the drawing room, told her to sit down beside him at his desk and laid before her all the details of his household, and when he mentioned casually what his income was, she gaped at him. 'But Jake, that's a fortune—it's quite frightening!'

'No, my dear; this house costs a lot to keep up and by the time we've deducted household expenses and a dozen and one other things, there's not a great deal over.' He pulled a sheet of paper towards her. 'See for yourself.'

She looked it over carefully because she could see that he expected her to do so, but even then there seemed to be a great deal of money over.

'So you see, my dear,' he was leaning back comfortably in his chair, 'if you should overspend your allowance you will not have to worry about it.'

Annis thought privately that she would have to be wildly extravagant even if she spent the whole of the generous allowance he gave her and said so, but he only laughed. 'Well, supposing we go to den Haag and do some shopping? We should give a dinner party soon, you know, and I want you to have a dress worthy of your lovely face.'

He had spoken lightly and she didn't allow herself to believe that he meant it. 'Who will come?' she asked.

'Mama, Elsa if she is back from her holiday and Adriaan with her of course, a handful of aunts and uncles, one or two of my friends who will be your friends too, I hope. Waldo and Olympia, perhaps? Shall we say twelve?'

'I shall be scared stiff!'

He shook his head. 'You're not easily scared, Annis, and I should know.'

They had their tea round the log fire in the small sitting room, and Annis, going upstairs to change her dress afterwards, sighed for the day which had seemed so brief and happy.

Schudderbeurs was full, but there was a table for them, ready in a corner of the restaurant while they sat cosily by the open hearth, sipping their drinks. The lights were dim, and the candles in their brass candlesticks on each table cast a mellow light; the murmur of talk around them and the faint smell of good food coming from the kitchen beyond, all combined to create a welcoming atmosphere. They sat down presently while Mevrouw Bouteka hovered discreetly and Annis, eating the delicious food, relaxed under the influence of Jake's quiet talk and the good wine, and forgetting her problems, chattered back to him, not noticing the gleam in his dark eyes.

And it was even better later that week. Jake had come home in the evening, walking into the small sitting room where she was sitting with Mike, conning her Dutch lessons. His quiet 'Hullo, Annis,' brought her to her feet and then sent her flying to him. His plaster had gone, a stout stick was all there was to show for his injury. Annis had caught his arm. 'Jake—oh, Jake, how lovely, how absolutely super! Why didn't you tell me it was to be today? And so soon?'

'Is it so important?' His dark eyes bored into hers, then he laughed. 'Well, perhaps it is—I shall be able to drive again.'

Which wasn't the answer she had hoped for. She

said: 'How nice,' rather crossly and asked him his plans for the next day.

'We'll go to den Haag,' he told her, 'and do some shopping—we'll share the driving, too. I know you haven't a licence yet, but I daresay if we're stopped I'll be able to explain.'

'But I don't think ...' began Annis.

'If you can drive a jeep in Spitzbergen, you can drive the Bristol on our excellent roads,' he told her in a no-nonsense voice which left her without argument. 'We must get your licence as quickly as possible, I'll tell Cor to see to it; your car will be delivered any day now.'

'My car?' queried Annis faintly.

'A Mini—you must have something to get about in when I'm not around.'

'Jake, how lovely! Thank you.' She wanted to throw her arms around his neck and hug him, instead she kissed him sedately on one cheek. He accepted this milk and water salute calmly enough, merely begging her to remember to drive on the right side of the road. His casual manner reminded her strongly of Freddy at his most brotherly.

The day in den Haag was perfect; Jake had driven the car out of Goes and on to the main road to Rotterdam and then pulled into a layby and told Annis to take the wheel, and when she protested he contrived to make her feel that his leg was being troublesome. 'But I daresay I can manage to drive through Rotterdam,' he told her soothingly, 'and den Haag is no distance from there.'

She had been terrified to start with and then, once

she had got the feel of the Bristol, she had begun to enjoy herself. By the time they had reached Rotterdam, she was almost sure that she could have driven through that city and she was quite prepared to do so, but Jake asured her that his leg was perfectly all right and they changed places again. She was glad of it really, for the traffic was heavy and the city confusing to a stranger. Jake knew his way well enough, though, and once clear of the outskirts, let the car slide ahead of the other traffic. He was a fast driver, but a safe one; Annis settled back in her seat, enjoying herself.

They had parked in the city's centre and had lunch and then Jake had taken her to a boutique in a narrow side street. He had spoken to the shop assistant who had disappeared with a smile and a nod and returned a few minutes later with an armful of gowns, to hold up each one in turn for Annis's inspection.

They were all equally lovely; silks and chiffons and crêpe-de-chines, and every colour of the rainbow. Annis instantly wished for every one of them but after a first inspection asked to try on a pearl grey silk jersey.

'Why do you choose that?' demanded Jake.

'Well, it's pretty and it won't date, you know . . .'

'My dear girl, we're not buying it for posterity, just for the dinner party. Here, let me . . .'

He got up from the elegant little chair he had sat in. 'The green,' he declared, 'and that cream thing with the lace. Try them both on.'

So she had tried them in turn, secretly delighted with his choice and quite horrified at the price when she discovered the tickets. The green crêpe-de-chine was exactly the shade of her eyes and fitted perfectly, and the cream was just as pretty, its chiffon folds edged with lace. Jake, inspecting them both in turn nodded. 'Have both,' he told her.

'But Jake ...'

He smiled and spoke to the saleswoman and went back to his little chair and presently, carrying an elegant dress box, they left the shop. 'Well,' said Annis, 'they're lovely, absolutely divine, but haven't I spent more than my allowance?'

'You haven't spent any of your allowance. I'll make you a present of them.'

'Jake, thank you!' She stopped to look at him. 'You are a dear ...'

He didn't answer her, only looked at her with faint mockery so that she went rather red. 'You'll need shoes,' he said after a silence she would have liked to break. 'There's a good shop in the next street.'

She forgot the awkward little moment in the excitement of choosing the shoes and later they had driven home in great spirits and spent the rest of the evening after dinner, in the drawing room, with Mike between them, laughing a great deal over Annis's attempts at holding a conversation in Dutch.

The dinner party was fixed for the following week and Annis spent anxious hours closeted with Katrina, frequently interrupted by calls for Cor to help out with translation. She was determined to make a success of this, her first attempt at entertaining, and since Jake had said carelessly that she could arrange whatever menu she wanted, she spent a good deal of time browsing through cook-books and reading recipes. And when she wasn't doing that she was crouched over the desk in the library, muttering away at suitable Dutch phrases with which to entertain her guests. She tried them out on Jake each evening at dinner and he, with a decided twinkle in his eyes, pronounced her progress quite remarkable.

She decided to wear the green crêpe-de-chine after trying on both dresses at least three times, and then, dressed far too soon, went downstairs. Jake came in as she reached the hall, but beyond a brief: 'Hullo, that's nice,' he said nothing but went straight upstairs, completely destroying her self-satisfaction. She wasn't a vain girl, but standing in front of the pier-glass in her room she had known that she looked just about as dishy as any girl could; the dress was exactly right, her hair, newly washed, wreathed her pretty face and danced in soft curls on her shoulders, the pearls glowed on her neck and her make-up had repaid the time she had taken over it. To have all this dismissed as 'nice' with barely a glance to justify such a poor compliment annoyed her very much. She swept into the drawing room and poured herself a glass of sherry and tossed it off. By the time Jake got downstairs, very elegant in his dinner jacket, she had a splendid colour and a slight headache. He took one look at her as he came in and asked: 'Have another sherry, Annis?'

She gave him a defiant look. 'I'm nervous,' she told him as he came over with her drink. But he didn't give it to her at once; he bent his head and kissed her gently first.

'No need,' he said in a voice as gentle as his kiss, 'you'll outshine every woman in sight.'

He put the glass in her hand and went to fetch his own drink, and presently began to tell her of his day.

Mevrouw van Germert arrived ahead of everyone else, sailing into the room, splendidly attired in dark blue velvet. And if I didn't know her, thought Annis, watching her regal progress, I'd be terrified of her. As it was her mother-in-law kissed her warmly, told her that she was a beautiful girl and then went to offer a cheek to her son.

'You make a handsome pair,' she pronounced. 'Annis, that is a charming dress. And you, Jake, how is your leg progressing?'

'Splendidly, Mama. You're looking very handsome yourself.'

His mother nodded her regal head. 'Thank you, my dear.' She accepted a glass of sherry and sat down. 'Annis, come and sit beside me and tell me what you have been doing. I hear from Jake that you are making tremendous progress with your Dutch.'

Annis blushed faintly. It was nice of Jake to praise her to his mother, especially when she wasn't there. She said now: 'Well, I'm doing my best. Jake found me a wonderful teacher, Mevrouw Pette ...'

Which started Mevrouw van Germert off on a rather rambling tale about that lady which lasted until the first of the guests arrived.

Olympia and Waldo came last of all and Annis, seizing an opportunity when everyone else was talking, whispered urgently: 'Olympia, there's something I want to ask you when I get a chance—before you go.'

Olympia studied her face. 'Of course. It's important,

isn't it? I can see that. There's bound to be a chance later on.'

The dining room looked rather grand. Annis had chosen to have an enormous white tablecloth falling to the ground, its pristine whiteness showing off silver and glass and beautiful Delft china. She had arranged the flowers herself, a low bowl of bronze chrysanthemums and yellow roses, and flanked it by silver candelabra, their lighted candles casting a soft glow over the table. She felt a little upsurge of pride as they seated themselves; the women's pretty dresses and the men's austere black and white were so exactly right in the dignified old room. She saw Jake's eyes on her from the head of the table and smiled at him before turning to Oom Karel, sitting on one side of her. He was a nice old man, she had only spoken to him for a few minutes at her wedding, but now she saw the chance to put a few questions, discreet of course, about Jake. But Oom Karel, although he regaled her with a dozen tales about the family, hardly mentioned him. And the uncle on her other side, still a little austere in his manner until he got to know her better, kept to generalities.

She ate her way through her carefully thought out menu; artichoke hearts with garlic sauce, tender, juicy little steaks with peppercorns and in a cream and brandy sauce, served with fennel and tiny pommes frites and to follow these, a soufflé glacé, pleased to see that their guests were enjoying what was on their plates. She rose from the table a little flushed with triumph and the excellent wine Jake had chosen, and indeed, in the drawing room the ladies of the party

were quick to gather round her and compliment her.
She poured coffee with a hand which shook just a little
with the excitement of it all and wondered, as she
made polite conversation with aunts and cousins, when
she would have the opportunity to get Olympia alone.
But Olympia's pink gown was almost invisible at the
other end of the room, surrounded by several ladies
of the party, and Annis, talking painstaking Dutch to
Tante Wilhelmina, gave up for the moment.

Her chance came later; the men had joined them
and the company had settled down into little groups,
comfortably exchanging gossip. Annis, with a glance at
Olympia, seated herself on a small sofa a little apart
and was quickly joined by her.

'Well?' asked Olympia, not wasting time.

'I've no time to explain and I expect you'll find it a
funny question. Who's Nina?'

Her companion didn't answer at once, then: 'Have
you asked Jake?'

'Yes, but he keeps putting it off and now I don't
like to ask any more, but I must know ... One of his
cousins at the wedding told me ...'

'That silly ...' Olympia's fine eyes expressed her
opinion better than any words. 'She's a nasty creature,
always making trouble for the fun of it. I suppose
everyone thought he'd marry Nina—oh, it was years
ago now. She went to America, but she came back last
year sometime ...' Olympia saw the look on Annis's
face and hurried on: 'No, don't worry, she doesn't
mean a thing—he's had girl-friends before and since,
but never serious. We thought he'd never marry.' She
paused. 'Perhaps I shouldn't have told you.'

'I asked you to,' Annis reminded her, 'and I'm glad I know. Now I'll know what to say to the abominable Ria next time I meet her, though I hope I never shall.'

Olympia giggled. 'She's ghastly, isn't she? And the trouble is that sometimes there's a grain of truth in what she says and she manages to twist it.'

'Well, she'd better not try it on me,' said Annis fiercely, and switched on a smile as Tante Beatrix and Tante Coralie, who seemed to do everything together, bore down upon them. She saw Jake looking at her from the far end of the room, his brows drawn together in a frown; perhaps she had been sitting too long with Olympia. She gave her new friend a conspirator's wink and started an animated, impossible to understand conversation with Tante Beatrix.

She must have imagined the frown, she decided, listening to Jake's comments on the evening after the last guest had gone, and then drew a sharp breath at his voice, a little cool now: 'And what were you asking Olympia so earnestly, Annis? Or is it a secret I may not share?'

She let out the breath. 'Well, no—it's not a secret, not mine, anyway, and it's you who don't want to share it with me, so I asked Olympia about Nina. Ever since that cousin of yours ...'

'I must admire you for your persistence, Annis, even if it is wasted on something as trivial.' His voice held mockery although he was smiling. On second thoughts she wasn't sure if she liked the smile, but she went on sturdily:

'I can't see any reason why you couldn't have told me yourself. At least, there is one reason, of course.

Perhaps you're still—still ...'

'In love with Nina?' he finished for her smoothly.
'Do you really suppose I would marry you if that had
been the case, Annis?'

'Well, I can't see why not,' she said matter-of-factly.
'If she wouldn't have you and I was ...' She paused,
at a loss for words.

'Nina and I, you and Ola,' he said softly. 'So that's
it, that's what you're thinking, isn't it?'

'Yes.'

He started towards her and then stopped as the telephone rang. As he lifted the receiver he said: 'We need
to talk, you and I, my dear,' and then became totally
absorbed in what was being said to him. Finally he
spoke briefly, hung up and said: 'I have to go at
once—don't wait up, it may be a long job.'

He had gone before she could utter and when she
went into the hall Cor was there, ready to open the
door for his master. Annis watched Jake go without a
glance in her direction, and then bade Cor a quiet
goodnight and went upstairs. But not to sleep.

And in the morning when she got downstairs, it was
to find Cor waiting with a message from Jake to say
that he might not be back for lunch.

'What happened, Cor?' She tried not to sound anxious. 'An accident?'

'Yes, Mevrouw—a bad one on the main road. They
have been very busy at the hospital, the doctor was
there most of the night, he came back early to shave
and eat his breakfast and went back within the hour.'

She sat down and ate her solitary breakfast, took
Mike for a walk and then, unable to settle to her

lessons, went down to the kitchen, a vast old-fashioned place in which all the mod cons had been installed without spoiling its charm. Here she sat down at the scrubbed wooden table and set about the business of discussing the day's meals with Katrina and the cook, a rather slow business still, although she was learning fast.

When she had mastered this task she asked in her slow Dutch: 'Is there any shopping?'

There was—not much, fruit from the greengrocers next to Hema's, if she would be so kind.

Annis, restless, was only too glad to have something to do until it was time for Mevrouw Pette to give her her lesson. She fetched the corduroy jacket which matched the grey skirt she was wearing, found a basket and walked into the town. She wouldn't think about Jake, she told herself as she went, and then thought of no one else, so that she didn't bother overmuch about what she was buying. It was a good thing that the greengrocer knew that she was Doctor van Germert's wife and saw to it that only the very best of his goods were sold to her.

She had time to spare and the way home past the Raadhuis and the church, although longer, was prettier. She had rounded the market square and was half way past the church when a man got out of a car parked on the side of the road and started towards her. It wasn't until he was really close that she noticed him and came to an abrupt halt, her face suddenly white.

'Ola?' she asked in astonishment.

He looked even more handsome than she had remembered and well dressed too, and the smile he gave her was the old charming smile, only it didn't quicken her pulse one beat. When he held out his hand she took it reluctantly.

'This is a surprise.' She spoke just as reluctantly in a stiff voice.

'Yes? I had business in Rotterdam. I flew from Norway yesterday and the first thing I have done is to come here and see you, my darling.'

'I'm not your darling,' declared Annis roundly, 'I'm Jake's wife.'

He shrugged his shoulders. 'Oh, that—a marriage of convenience. How could it be anything else for you? And he such a cold fish.'

'He's nothing of the kind,' she said hotly and when he smiled again: 'How did you know where I was?'

'So easy—I have merely to ask where Jake lives, and then I ask, oh, so casually, where you are, and I am told ...'

'Who told you?'

He opened his blue eyes wide. 'My darling Annis, I telephoned a man from the station who was on holiday in Norway.'

Her eyes flashed green fire. 'Indeed?' Her voice was icy. 'Well, I have to go; I have an appointment.'

'Coffee first?' He was using all his old charm again. 'There is so much that I have to say to you.'

'No coffee, and there's nothing to say, Ola. Goodbye.'

She walked away trying not to hurry, because then he might think that she was running away from him, which, she admitted to herself, she was. When she got back home she was breathless and shaking and Cor, who had been in the hall when she went in, said at once: 'Mevrouw, you are ill? What has happened?'

Annis mumbled something or other and went up to her room and shut the door before going over to the dressing table and sitting down before it. Her knees felt weak and her still pale face stared back at her from the mirror.

'Oh, why couldn't Jake have been there?' she whispered to her reflection. 'He'd have known what to say and do.' But perhaps he wouldn't have said anything, she thought unhappily; she supposed he still thought that she loved Ola, he might even have stood aside and given Ola a second chance—but he was married, or perhaps not any more? She sat for a little while feeling tired and drained, not even thinking, until it was time for her to go down for her lesson with Mevrouw Pette, but she, poor lady, got no sense out of her during the next hour. She looked hard at Annis's abstracted face and ventured: 'Perhaps you have been working too hard, Mevrouw van Germert. We will cut short our lesson, I think, and you will not do your homework, only read the papers if you wish and remember to speak Dutch as often as possible.'

She went away, shaking her head at her own stupidity in letting Annis work too hard at her lessons.

The rest of the day was awful. Jake didn't come home for lunch and Annis, in a fever that Ola would come knocking at the door, and yet afraid to go out in case she met him again, mooned around the house and then took Mike into the garden until it was time for tea, which she drank with an ear cocked for the sound of Jake's key in the door.

It wasn't until almost seven o'clock that he came home, and then he looked so tired that she had no heart to tell him about meeting Ola. He went upstairs almost at once and when he joined her in the sitting room it was to tell her that he would have to go out again without delay. 'A patient I should have seen this afternoon,' he explained. 'He's coming to my consulting rooms, and afterwards I may call in at the hospital again. Don't wait up for me.'

She said, 'Very well,' in a quiet little voice, and added: 'Haven't you time to tell me what's happened?'

He smiled at her from his tired face. 'Not now, my dear, I must go.'

She nodded. 'Of course. I'll see that there's a Thermos of coffee and some sandwiches left for you.'

'You're a splendid wife, Annis,' he told her as he went.

As she heard the front door close she got up and wandered to the window in time to see the Bristol shoot away. 'Not even time to kiss me,' she told Mike bitterly, 'but perhaps he doesn't want to.'

She ate a solitary dinner, then went back to the sitting room and picked up the newspaper she had been painstakingly trying to read. She was frowning over the small ads when she heard the front door bell and Cor going to the door. She knew who it was before Cor had opened the door to ask her if she would see a Mr Ola Julsen. She said yes at once, surprised to see that her hands, folding the newspaper, were quite steady.

Ola came in with a self-assurance she envied. 'Jake's not home?' He smiled. 'I do not need to ask, of course, I saw him leave the house. He will be away for the evening, I suppose. I hear that the hospital is very busy.'

'He'll be back at any moment,' said Annis. 'Why have you come?'

He smiled again and she thought irritably that he was always smiling—why hadn't she noticed that before? 'To see you, my darling girl.'

'I am not your darling girl, you're wasting your time, Ola. Please go.'

He didn't budge. 'Not until I have begged your forgiveness for the way in which I treated you, Annis, not until you say that I am forgiven. Oh, my dear, we could be so happy together, just the two of us.' He sat down. 'I do not believe that you and Jake are in love—you, who are so full of life and warmth and he so calm and cold, hardly noticing you. Ah, the times I could have knocked him down for the cool way he treated you.'

Annis was on her feet. 'You be quiet!' Her voice had risen with her temper. 'Who are you to talk of his treatment of me? What about your treatment? And what about your wife?'

He shrugged. 'A divorce—so easy. We could marry later if you wished.'

'I can think of nothing I would dislike more,' said Annis furiously. 'I think you're mad!' Her voice got a little too loud. 'Now for heaven's sake go before I throw something at you!'

She tugged the bell pull and Cor came so quickly

that she wondered if he had been just outside the door
—not listening, Cor would never do that, just staying
close by in case she should need him. He held the door
open without a word and Ola blew her a kiss and
with a shrug of his shoulders followed Cor into the
hall.

Annis stayed where she was for a few minutes, then
got up and went slowly out of the room. It was only
as she stood in the hall that she realised that the study
door was open and Jake was sitting at his desk, writing. She had no idea how long he had been there or if
he had heard anything, and unless Cor had gone down
the hall and looked he wouldn't have seen that he was
in the house again. He didn't look up until she was at
the door and had pushed it wide open and when he
did she had no idea if he knew or not; his face gave
nothing away.

She said in a quiet little voice: 'Ola was here.'

Jake put down his pen and looked up at her. 'Oh?
To see you, my dear?' He sounded only mildly interested.

'Yes.' She swallowed from a dry mouth. 'He wanted
me to go away with him; he said he was sorry for the
way he'd treated me, that he'd left his wife.'

Jake's dark eyes didn't leave her face. 'And he came
all this way to tell you that?'

She shook her head. 'At least, he said he'd had to
go to Rotterdam on business. He got your address from
someone he knew who'd been at the station.'

Jake nodded. 'And what did you say, Annis?'

'That I wouldn't go away, that I didn't want to ...'
She wanted to tell him that Ola meant nothing to her,

that he himself, sitting there looking quite grey with weariness, was the only man she would ever love. She opened her mouth to say so and then shut it again because of the bleak, unyielding look on his face.

'You were surprised to see him?'

'Of course I was—I didn't expect to see him again ever. I couldn't believe my eyes when I saw him this morning.'

His eyebrows rose a little. 'That too?'

She mumbled an explanation and went on: 'He came to the house just now ...'

'After you had met him this morning?' His cold voice implied that they had arranged it between them and she said sharply: 'You think I asked him to come?'

His eyes looked black and hard. 'The thought did cross my mind.'

Annis said loudly: 'You thought I would encourage him, that I told him to come, that I ...' She broke off and stood twisting the door handle to and fro in her hands. Then: 'You're busy, aren't you, I won't bother you now. Goodnight, Jake.'

She closed the door very quietly behind her and went upstairs.

At breakfast the next morning Annis, struggling to keep some kind of conversation going, painstakingly worked her way through the weather, Mike, and then the weather again, until his remote politeness stilled her tongue. He was getting up from the table when she burst out with: 'Jake, I do want to talk to you. I know you're busy, but couldn't you spare a few minutes now?'

He stood looking at her, large and powerful and rugged and apparently unruffled. His voice was mild. 'I think it might be better if we waited until we both feel calmer, when we can discuss the situation rationally.'

'But there isn't a situation, and I don't want to be rational!' cried Annis, almost in tears.

He turned away and she realised that he was furiously angry and hiding it.

'Which is exactly why we should wait until you have had time to become so.'

She had got up too, standing holding on to the back of her chair. 'Jake, I don't want any time, I only want to tell you ..'

He went to the door and opened it before he answered her. 'Not now.' And he went without another look at her.

Annis brushed away her tears with a furious hand, sat herself down and drank another cup of coffee without tasting any of it.

Presently she got up and crossed the hall to the library and sat down at the desk there. After several false starts she cast aside her intention to write the kind of letter she had meant to and instead took another sheet of paper and scribbled her feelings down just as she felt.

'Jake, I'm going away. It's no use me staying, because you don't believe me about Ola and I've been trying to tell you for weeks that I love you, but I don't suppose you'd believe that either—perhaps you don't want to. And if it's still Nina you want then for heaven's sake say so. I'm quite able to look after myself and who knows, I might get rational—if I do I'll let you know. Annis.'

She dashed this missive off with an angry pen and not bothering to read it through, put it in an envelope and left it on Jake's desk in his study. Even if he was coming back for lunch, she had plenty of time to go wherever she was going. She stood in the hall, wondering just where she should go and how, and a nasty little feeling of panic crept through her. She had no idea.

The matter was nicely solved for her by Cor, coming to look for her.

'The car the doctor ordered for you, Mevrouw—it has just arrived. Perhaps you would like to inspect it.'

She had forgotten about the car, and it seemed like a sign from heaven. She could use it to get away, but where to go? She smiled at Cor and while she was declaring her delight and saying that yes, she would come at once, she was thinking feverishly. Olympia? That wouldn't do, she couldn't implicate her, nor could she go to her mother-in-law. There wasn't anywhere else. The panic caught hold again until she remembered Schudderbeurs. Not too far away, quiet, and after all it was an hotel as well as a restaurant. She found herself on the doorstep looking at a Mini, exactly the same colour as the Bristol. It was a beautiful little car; as she examined it she felt sick with misery. Everything could have been so wonderful; she had thought that once Jake's leg had recovered completely everything would have come right between them, but it had made no difference, his manner hadn't changed one iota from his usual casual friendliness. She dimly heard Cor ask: 'Mevrouw, are you ill? You are so pale.'

She managed a smile. 'I'm excited, Cor, that's all. Could it stay here for a while, I'd like to examine it presently.'

'Of course, Mevrouw. Your licence hasn't arrived yet?'

'No, but I've got my British one with me, though that's no use—or is it?' She didn't wait for him to reply but went on: 'When Mevrouw Pette comes, could we have coffee right away, not at the end of the lesson as we usually do?'

'Of course, Mevrouw.'

She smiled at him and ran upstairs to her room, her mind full of the idea which was getting clearer every minute. She would tell Cor that she was going to take the Mini for a very short run, and then just go. Jake would know that she was all right because of the letter. She pulled a small case out of the clothes closet and packed a few things haphazardly; enough for a week, she decided, and gave a tearful giggle. 'I'll be rational by then,' she said out loud, and then burst into tears.

She had done things to her face by the time Mevrouw Pette was due to arrive, so that although she was a little pale, there was no trace of tears. She had never been so clever at her lessons; Mevrouw Pette was full of praise for her hard work, congratulating herself silently for having been lenient with her pupil over the last few days. 'You will be speaking as well as any of us very shortly,' she promised, 'and think how proud of you the doctor will be.'

Annis agreed woodenly, suggested that the lesson might end a little early as she had one or two things to do before lunch and bade her teacher goodbye. The house was quiet as she went upstairs. Everyone would be in the kitchen for half an hour or so. She changed into a jersey dress and the long coat matching it, put on a pair of high-heeled shoes, quite impractical in the circumstances but wonderful for her morale, and ran downstairs.

Cor looked doubtful about her taking the car and wanted to come with her. 'Just a short run,' she told him breathlessly, I'll be quite all right.'

'And is there any message for the doctor if he should return early, Mevrouw?'

'No—no, thank you, Cor.' She avoided his doubtful eye, kissed Mike's great head and went to the door, conscious that Cor's eyes were on the case.

'Shoes,' she told him, 'for mending, you know.' She was away before he could answer her. He watched her start the little car and disappear round the corner before he closed the door, frowning. There was something not quite right ...

CHAPTER NINE

ANNIS drove the Mini carefully through Goes and over the Zeeland Brug to the outskirts of Zierikzee where she turned off along the brick dyke road which would take her to Schudderbeurs. It was clouding over now, the sun hidden behind thick ribbons of cloud, and although the little car was warm, she shivered. She turned again presently, into the narrow lane which would take her the short distance to the hotel. It was very quiet everywhere and she wished suddenly that she was back home in Goes. Perhaps she should have stayed with Jake, although she didn't think that that would have been possible. They had reached a point in their relationship when they had either to talk or finish—and Jake wouldn't talk.

The hostelry was as quiet as the countryside around it and there were only a couple of cars parked on the sweep before its door. She set the Mini tidily beside them and went inside.

Mevrouw Bouteka came to meet her. 'Mevrouw van Germert—what a surprise, and how nice to see you ...' She peered over Annis's shoulder. 'And the doctor? You come for lunch, perhaps?'

'Yes, please, at least just me—the doctor's not with me.' Annis followed her into the restaurant and sat down at a small table. 'Just something light, please, I'm not hungry.'

'An omelette, with a salad on the side and perhaps a glass of sherry first? Or coffee?'

'Sherry, please, and coffee later.' Annis settled in her chair, suddenly tired, resolutely trying not to think. She felt better when she had had lunch, and it was over her coffee that she asked Mevrouw Bouteka: 'Have you a room? I'd like to stay here for a day or two—my case is in the car.'

Not a muscle of Mevrouw Bouteka's pleasant face changed. 'But of course, Mevrouw. We aren't busy now at the end of the season, we have several rooms. Your case shall be taken up for you.'

'Thank you—I'm not sure for how long.' She followed Mevrouw Bouteka's brisk tread up the stairs and into a pleasant room on the first floor and sat down to wait while her case was fetched. Unpacking took no time at all, and it was too unpleasant outside to go for a walk. She lay down on the bed and presently went to sleep.

When she woke up it was four o'clock; at least she could go down and have a cup of tea. The restaurant was deserted and she sat down by the open hearth and picked up a magazine. But it was in Dutch and in her present state it was too much effort to try and understand any of it. Her head was full of Jake and nothing else. She couldn't imagine being without him and thinking about him had started to dissolve the hard knot of tears she had so resolutely held at bay; the tears began to trickle down her cheeks, faster than she could wipe them away. And that was how Mevrouw Bouteka found her presently, and she, being a wise little woman, said nothing but fetched a tray of tea,

put another log on the fire, made some cheerful remark about the drabness of the day, then went away
again. In her office she sat thoughtfully for a few
minutes and then went in search of her husband.
When she came back, she closed the door carefully behind her and lifted the telephone receiver. She knew
Jake's number, she was a methodical person and had
the names and addresses of all her regular visitors. She
was a discreet woman, but just now and then she considered that discretion should be cast to the four
winds.

Jake answered the phone, Annis's note still in his
hand. He had just come in and Cor, meeting him at
the door, had told him at once that Annis wasn't home.
'She's been gone for several hours,' said Cor worriedly.
'I took the liberty of telephoning round to the most
likely places ...'

'My friends in Middelburg?' interrupted Jake, white
about the mouth.

'Oh, yes, and Mevrouw van Germert your mother,
and your sister, and I rang Vlissingen and the Hoek ...'

The two men exchanged glances. 'Thank you, Cor.
I've been a fool.' Jake's voice was bitter. When the
telephone rang he snatched at the receiver and said
'Yes?' impatiently.

Cor watched the harsh lines of his face soften and
disappear and let out a sigh of relief as Jake said: 'I'll
be over within the hour, Mevrouw Bouteka. Please
don't say anything to my wife. And thank you.'

He replaced the receiver slowly. 'My wife's at Schudderbeurs, Cor. She took the Mini. I can't go immediately; there's that urgent case I must see, but I should

be back in half an hour. Stay near the phone and let me know if there's anything—I'll be at the hospital.'

He was gone, looking suddenly ten years younger.

Annis had gone for a walk after all, wrapped in an old coat of Mevrouw Bouteka's. The grey skies had turned to rain, a fine rain with a chilly wind, but she hardly noticed, it was something to do and it passed the long day.

When she went down to dinner the restaurant was almost empty, as it was early yet. Two couples on the further side of the room were almost hidden by the centre chimney and Annis, sitting on its further side, was well hidden. Mevrouw Bouteka had wished her a good evening, put a cup of coffee on the table beside her and gone again, back to the table in front of the little bar, where she sat when the tables were occupied, doing her accounts.

Annis took a sip of coffee and then, lost in thought, forgot it. She was unable to think sensibly any more, her head was awash with silly daydreams and longings and regrets. They occupied her thoughts so completely that she didn't see Jake come in.

He sat down beside her and took her hand in his and held it fast. He said very softly: 'Hullo, darling.'

Annis sat staring at him, her face even whiter than it had been. She made a futile attempt to pull her hand free and cast around in her bewildered head for something to say; equally futile, for all she came up with was a whispered: 'How did you know?'

His smile warmed the cold inside her although he still looked tired to death. 'I didn't,' he told her. 'I was trying to decide where to look for you when Mevrouw Bouteka telephoned.'

'She did? But why should she do that?'

His hand still enveloped hers, it felt very large and firm and she hoped that he would never let her own hand go. 'Most people like to see the path of true love running smoothly,' he told her.

'Oh,' said Annis, and was glad when Mevrouw Bouteka joined them. She had been watching them for the last few minutes and had drawn her own conclusions.

'How nice to see you, Doctor van Germert. You will have a drink? And I hope you are staying for dinner?'

'Champagne cocktails, Mevrouw Bouteka, and yes, we should like to dine.' He took the menu she offered without releasing Annis's hand. 'I don't suppose you've had much to eat, my love. What would you like?'

She was suddenly put out; it seemed that all he could think of was dinner. Mevrouw Bouteka came back with their drinks and she heard Jake tell her that they wouldn't dine for another half an hour. 'We should like to sit here quietly,' he told her, and she being perceptive said instantly:

'Of course—we aren't busy. If you would like to order it shall be served in half an hour's time.'

Annis was staring down into her glass and he smiled a little. 'Some of your excellent fish, I think, for us both, perhaps an avocado first? We can leave the sweet for the moment, can we not? And champagne, please.'

When Mevrouw Bouteka had gone, he said: 'We have a great deal to say to each other, my dearest darling. Most of it can wait until we are home again, but I find myself quite unable to sit here without telling you that I love you.' His hand tightened on hers as she looked up at him. He went on quietly: 'I fell in love with you when you arrived at the station, you know, and then just as I began to think I was making some headway with you, Ola arrived so dramatically and swept you off your feet.'

Annis's green eyes were swimming with tears. 'But you didn't believe me—you thought I still loved him, and I tried to tell you and you wouldn't listen—and that beastly Nina ...'

He lifted her hand and kissed the palm gently. 'Nina, my darling, is of no account, a piece of my past which is of no possible importance.' He added with a twinkle: 'Just like Ola.'

Annis gave a sniff and then a shaky little laugh. 'I didn't know you loved me, Jake, darling Jake.'

'That's better. And I had no intention of telling you, not while I thought Ola was still such a menace.' He squeezed her hand. 'Drink up, sweetheart, it will give you an appetite.'

She felt the champagne giving her a lift, but she didn't need one now; suddenly life was glorious, she was so happy that she wanted to throw her arms round Jake's neck and kiss him. She could do that later, she told herself happily. Now she was content to sit here beside him, watching his dark, loved face and listening to him calling her his darling. She drank the rest of her champagne and said dreamily: 'Everything's wonderful. Jake, I shouldn't have had that drink.'

He laughed. 'It isn't the champagne, darling. Ah, here is our dinner.'

She had no idea what she ate, certainly she drank a little too much champagne, and when she protested all Jake would say was: 'After all, dearest, this is our wedding night.'

He covered her hand on the table and said: 'Eat your dinner, like a good girl, and we'll go home.'

So she ate obediently, looking up every now and then to find him looking at her with such love that she pinkened with delight, wishing the meal was over and they were home again. But Mijnheer Bouteka's cooking wasn't the sort one could hurry over and it seemed a long time before they had drunk their coffee and Jake said: 'Go and pack your bag, darling; someone will fetch it down for you while I pay the bill.'

She wanted to run up the staircase as fast as she could go, but she managed not to and when she came down a few minutes later she looked to be her usual serene self, only her eyes glowed with excitement.

They wished Mevrouw Bouteka goodbye and went out into the chilly evening to where the Bristol was standing, and just before she got in Jake kissed her swiftly. 'My God, I've been wanting to do that all the evening,' he said. 'We'll be home in less than half an hour.' He turned to look at her. 'My darling, promise me you'll never run away again—nothing quite so terrifying has ever happened to me in my whole life.'

She put a hand on his knee. 'I promise, Jake.'

He smiled briefly and started the engine and they hardly spoke again until he drew up outside the house in Goes. Cor must have been lying in wait for them; the door was thrown open with a great flourish and such a broad smile that Annis cried: 'Oh, Cor, how nice to see you waiting!'

Jake spoke quietly to him and he nodded and took

her coat as Jake took her arm. 'The little sitting room,' he murmured. There's a fire there and Cor will bring us some coffee presently.'

He shut the door behind them and stood leaning against it, watching her. Annis turned round and ran back across the room. 'Jake, oh Jake, I do love you so. I think it's always been you—when you rescued Harald and broke your leg—I didn't know then, only I was so miserable about it. How could I have been so blind and silly?'

He opened his arms and caught her fast. 'My darling girl, I believe we're going to be very happy, we've done so much together, haven't we? Although there's a lot we have to catch up on. This, for instance!'

He kissed her long and hard and she sighed and wormed her way a little closer.

'I expect we'll have to practise quite often,' she said, and kissed him back.

'Oh, undoubtedly,' said Jake, 'and there's no time like the present, don't you agree, sweetheart?'

And Annis agreed.

FREE
Harlequin
romance
catalogue

This catalogue
provides you
with a complete listing of all the
titles currently available through

Harlequin Reader Service

Harlequin's Collection . . .

Many of these exciting romance novels have not been available since their original publication.

Harlequin Presents...

Stories of elegance and sophistication . . .

Harlequin Romances

. . . and be sure not to miss any of these exciting novels.

Don't miss any of these exciting titles.

Complete and mail this coupon today!

Don't let this chance pass you by!

And there's still *more* love in

Harlequin Presents...